A Lethal Investment
...to make a killing.

by

Stephen Barrett

About the Author

Stephen Barrett has spent more than thirty-five years working in the financial services industry in the UK, Germany and across Europe. Writing has been his passion for many years, and *A Lethal Investment* is his second novel, following on from *A Casual Temptation*, based on the many diverse experiences gained in his long career.

Stephen lives in Düsseldorf, Germany, and spends as much time as possible in sunny Worthing, which is still very much his home.

Dedication

I dedicate this book to my wife, Anja, for her ongoing support and letting me write when other chores need doing, and my nephew, Oliver, for his amazing input and fantastic ideas in making some of the passages in *A Lethal Investment* come alive.

Author's Note

In the thirty-five years I have been working in the financial services sector, the development of IT-based tools to digitalise and streamline processes has been constantly accelerating. None have impacted the credit process as much as automated credit-decisioning tools. For a long time it was deemed unethical to automate credit decisions – having machines decide on whether a bank's customer was worthy of receiving a loan seemed a no-go. Today, automated credit-decisioning tools are standard procedure for both private and corporate customers.

Along with the development and deployment of such tools, new and clever methods to defraud banks by manipulating these systems have been created. Fraudsters have learnt to play the game, constantly probing and testing the limits of such systems. Nowadays, identity theft, the setting up of fake accounts, and manipulating financial data to boost the credit score with the intent of defrauding financial institutions are commonplace. The damage in terms of pounds, dollars and euros inflicted by such fraudulent activities is hard to estimate, but it runs into billions.

Apart from fraudulent attacks from outsiders (external fraud), which banks combat with more and sharper software solutions, nowadays incorporating AI, the biggest threat comes from insiders (internal fraud). Despite vastly improved safety measures, stringent policies and ever-increasing compliance supervision, the potential damage that can be caused by a bank's own employees can never be underestimated.

Names like Nick Leeson and Jérôme Kerviel are just a couple that made the headlines. The damage these two traders were able to inflict was staggering. In the case of Nick Leeson, his rogue trading activities in 1995 resulted in losses amounting to GBP 827 million. It meant the end of Barings Bank, founded in 1762 and one of the oldest merchant banks in England. In 2008, Jérôme Kerviel was able to build up a portfolio of unauthorised trades to the value of roughly EUR 50 billion, resulting in a mind-blowing loss of EUR 4.9 billion.

Reality is often so bizarre; you just can't make it up.

1

"He says he wants to buy a bank." Zuki turns to me, switching the phone from one ear to the other with a frown knotting itself into place on her brow.

I turn from the mirror by the door where I've been trying to tie the knot of my new silk tie. "What?"

Zuki is listening intently. Alexis does have this trait of talking and laughing at the same time, making him totally incomprehensible. I can hear his loud booming voice echoing out of the phone's straining speaker. She looks across at me, her face full of questions.

"He says he'll be buying it with their own money, so it's a good deal," she says, translating Alexis's garbled words into plain text.

I shrug, dismissing the conversation, and return to my tie. I have grown accustomed to these weird and wonderful outbursts. Alexis does this often enough. He's like a kid, seeing and wanting new toys all the time.

"Buy a bank?" I murmur. Ridiculous.

The rest of the conversation is lost to me since they have switched to speaking Greek.

I shift my position so I can watch Zuki in the mirror. She's sitting on the other side of the bed. She's all ready for this event, our official debut. Once I have worked out how to tie the knot on this bloody thing I'll be ready, too. It's the first time I've worn a tie in over a year, and I've forgotten how to tie a decent knot. For years I used to wear a tie every day, but not anymore. I loosen up the crooked knot and start again.

It would be easier if I didn't spend half the time watching Zuki in the mirror. But I can't help it, and I still can't believe this beautiful woman has chosen to fall in love with me. Zuki always says she's a *Heinz 57*, referring to her mother of American Japanese descent and her father, a Greek Cypriot. But whatever ingredients went into the recipe, the outcome is simply amazing. Zuki has the thick dark hair of her mother and the olive-coloured skin of her father. She has amazing eyes, with a chestnut-coloured ring around her pupils that captivates you if you gaze into her eyes long enough – that's if she lets you, for she has a Greek temperament: strong-willed, passionate and fearless.

And she is carrying my child. Four months gone now since she told me, the bulge now growing perceptibly. She's twice as beautiful as when I first set eyes on her in August last year. So much has changed in such a short timespan. I do a quick calculation. Just over a year since I left the country in a hurry, with a canvas holdall full of money and a desperate hope of being able to start a new life. Good lord, how my life *has* changed in such a brief period of time, but not as I expected. I'd never have imagined, not in my wildest dreams, that my life could change so drastically – and it isn't just Zuki.

"Neil? Zuki? Are you coming?" My mother's voice from the hall downstairs puts an end to my reverie. I look across to Zuki, who's just ending the call with Alexis.

"He says enjoy the party and the holiday, and then he wants us back in Cyprus as soon as possible. And he's serious about buying into this bank." She gives me a long, appraising look. "Nice," is her verdict. "Such a handsome man have I found," she adds, a smile spreading across her immensely kissable lips. Reading my mind, she comes over to me, straightens the tie and gives me a long kiss.

2

This is our party. A family do with friends, relatives and neighbours. The kind of event that used to make me cringe, but not today. I'm happy to be home, and I am proud to officially present Zuki to my mum, my brother, the few relatives who have made the trip to Worthing, and the even fewer friends, with their girlfriends and wives, that I have left. Uncle George declined the invitation, but that doesn't surprise me. I can't blame him for not coming. After all, I did nick his yacht and sail it to Ostend, abandoning it there. I even welcome our nosy neighbours, who I don't care about but Mum insisted on inviting. I want them all to see Zuki.

But it's not just the joy of showing off Zuki that makes me feel so elated, it's also my first time back to Worthing in over a year. And that in itself is an occasion I wouldn't have imagined possible – at least not so soon. I haven't mentioned to anyone that I entered the country under my new name, Jordan Epica, and with my new Cypriot passport. I have no idea what would have happened if I'd presented my real passport, but I wasn't going to take the risk. I have to assume that I'm still *persona non grata* in the UK. But *Jordan Epica*? I still can't get used to it.

It's not a name I would have chosen myself, but according to Alexis if you need a new identity then it has to be a proper identity and not just a name in a passport. Jordan has a driving licence, medical insurance, school and university certificates. Jordan has a past, a present and a future. And equipped with that identity, so do I. Besides, *what's in a name?* That's what Alexis had said to me when he handed me the new passport. It also just happened to be a name he had available. False identities don't come ten a penny, he'd explained. They are elaborate to construct and accordingly cost a small fortune, even for Alexis. And so, despite my sincere gratitude, I'm stuck with a stupid name.

We go down the creaky old stairs, the carpet worn thin on the steps and the paint on the walls faded and cracked, where in the small hall my mum stands beaming at us. I think she's as much in love with Zuki as I am.

"Oh, Zuki, you look lovely," she says. No mention of how nice I look. Mum doesn't so much as glance at me, but that doesn't matter. I only agreed to this party to please my mum. Pleasing my mum is a duty I felt I had to fulfil. That's not quite true – I *wanted* to fulfil, especially after the events of last year.

My mum, now in her mid-sixties, never had an easy life. How could she, married to a man like my father? She was – *is* – the complete opposite to him: kind, loving and caring. Bringing up four boisterous boys in a family environment dominated by my father's harsh regime, she still managed to create a loving home for us. I think it was a relief to her when my dad passed away, struck down prematurely by a heart attack. She blossomed after that, creating a new and pleasant life for herself. She has her silver-grey hair short now, and I can't help but feel that she's shrunk even more since I last saw her. But that doesn't matter. Not today. Mum's all smiles, happy to have us home, covering up her disappointment in me.

"So lovely," my mum repeats, tears of joy welling up.

In fact, Zuki has made a special effort but, and that's the effect she always manages to create, it's never over the top. Whatever she wears, it always seems so natural to her. In deference to her Japanese American heritage, she's selected a kimono-inspired blue and white silk summer dress. The blue and white colours are in turn a reference to her Greek, or – to be precise – Greek Cypriot heritage. I forewarned her that the subtleties will be lost on the assembled Britishers, but she just smiled.

The effect is, as always, pure admiration. Zuki is stunning whatever she wears. She's a natural beauty. Whilst aware of it, she never shows that she knows it. She's the least conceited person I've ever met. Me, I could go naked and nobody would notice. Today, I am just an accessory.

"Good luck," I whisper into Zuki's ear. She nudges me in the side, smiling at me.

Mum goes ahead and we follow her, in a tiny procession, into the lounge where the nosiest guests are sitting and standing, waiting. I have to smile as I see how many guests have crammed themselves into my mother's lounge, leaving just a narrow path for us to squeeze through. The lounge isn't big at the best of times, and for today's special occasion Ben and his helpers have pushed the armchairs into the corners and moved the heavy coffee table into the front room. Big smiles on beaming faces, and amidst plenty of oohs and aahs, we make our appearance. I can't help but think it's a bit how royalty must feel. But Zuki's the focus of all assembled. I get to shake hands as we squeeze past in single file, but the attention I'm given is brief as eyes revert immediately back to Zuki.

I can only guess what my mother and Ben, my brother, have told the guests ahead of this event, given my nefarious deeds. The shock of my involvement in a major fraud case the year before and my sudden disappearance was a major scandal in such a small community.

But the shame and disgrace I brought upon myself, and my family, was alleviated by my subsequent cooperation with the British authorities. I think that's the tale my mum and Ben have spun over the last few months. I understand – it's a version of the truth that's better suited to their circumstances. I think they should have left it at that and buried the whole thing deep as soon as the scandal became old news, but both Mum and Ben can't leave an opportunity like that unexploited. They just had to expand and beef up the story, revelling to some degree in the dubious glory. And so, a tale has developed – a tale of me being a secret agent, almost as if I only joined the gang of fraudsters in order to spy on them. All on behalf of the government, of course.

Little do they know, but I'm not going to spoil things. And neither is Zuki, who in fact knows every detail of what happened last year. A scheme Alexis and Michalis, her father, developed and implemented. She also knows the role I inadvertently came to play in its deployment. Zuki is fine with all that, but that's a different story and a different aspect of my wife's character. Oh, and there it is, that other little secret. Everybody assumes we *are* married, but we're not. We failed to do so. Not that we didn't want to ahead of coming over, but the logistics of creating a new identity hadn't included the prerequisite details needed to marry. Us becoming an item just hadn't figured at the time. Creating the missing details are work in progress. Alexis has initiated the process, including the necessary bribes to make the missing details happen. But there's one other problem: Zuki doesn't want to be Mrs Epica. She finds the name as stupid as I do. She wants to be Mrs Wilson. Neil Wilson being my real name. Accordingly, we have let everybody believe we are married, rings and all the other paraphernalia included, but we're not. Not quite a lie, but just not the truth either – I know it's confusing. If there's one thing I've learnt in the last year – or even longer, sometimes I can't remember when I started lying so smoothly – is that if you lie, lie well. Alexis always says, "Lie big." The bigger the lie, the more it will be believed. He should know, being an expert.

We move slowly through the ranks, shaking hands, nodding hellos, and I'm amazed at the amount of fresh flowers standing in vases that have been crammed into the lounge, standing on the mantelpiece, the windowsill and even on the shelves where Mum usually keeps her books and photo albums. I smile at the thought that flowers and guests seem to be competing for space to gawk at Zuki. It's a slow process through the lounge, out into the conservatory and finally into the garden, where a large marquee has been set up, just about fitting onto the lawn. The English weather is benign, too, for it's a sunny April day, some warmth already in the air and perfect for this fine occasion. We find our places and sit down, watching the faces watching us.

"Please, everyone, do sit down," I say once the embarrassment gets too much, and amidst smiles and laughter the spell breaks. To my relief, all assembled sit down and normal behaviour resumes. People start talking to each other rather than staring at Zuki. Zuki squeezes my hand and smiles a thanks at me.

In the brief moment of calm before the crazy ceremony begins, I cast a quick glance around. Ben and his helpers have managed to squeeze the big marquee in between the pear trees on the left and the apple trees on the right. My mother's garden, although bigger than Ben's, which is why we're having the party here, is by no means large. There's a tall, old flint stone wall at the rear and fences left and right. Out of the corner of my eye, I briefly glimpse a head peeking over next door's fence.

Zuki and I are sitting with our backs to the flint wall, looking towards the rear of the house and the conservatory. Through the dining room window, I can see plenty of activity going on in the dining room and kitchen. Ben's helpers, mainly friends, Mum's choir members and neighbours are busy getting the first course ready. He's got a caterer in, which at least means the food should be decent. In fact, I'm impressed with his organisation. He's managed to procure tables and chairs, covered in a fancy white elastic fabric in honour of this, our ceremonious celebration, and stuffed them into the uneven space under the marquee.

Now thirty people are sitting squeezed in tight, legs and arms rubbing. Cream-coloured place mats with fine tableware, crystal glasses and silver cutlery hired for the occasion are crammed onto the tables, and in the middle of each round table stands a large vase of flowers, too big given the available space and obstructing everyone's view. I smile as I see faces and torsos leaning sideways, talking around the vases. It's not what Zuki and I wanted, but Ben, or maybe Mum, insisted. I appreciate the effort Ben and Mum have made, but the effect is a bit on the comical side. Alexis would be smirking if he could see us now.

I scan the faces. I'm surprised at so many unfamiliar ones, and I can only assume my notoriety must have been an incentive to attend today's party. Half of the guests seem to be from my mother's choir group. The other half is a familiar assortment of old school friends, their wives and girlfriends, neighbours, and both sets of uncles and aunts on my mother's side – minus Uncle George, of course. Ben has taken it upon himself to be master of ceremonies and launches into a little speech. I cringe inwardly, fearing he's going to get carried away and embark on a potentially embarrassing account of my deeds one year ago. But fortunately, he keeps it brief.

"And so," he concludes, "Neil's adventures have ended and allowed him to return home with a jewel. And that jewel, Zuki, is you." Smarmy git, I think, but I smile back at him and squeeze Zuki's hand. She smiles her sweetest smile at him, too. I have to give it her, she's a good actress. "Let's raise our glasses to this wonderful couple," he says, and we all smile and beam at each other. Raising our glasses, we toast and sip the cheap champagne Ben has bought. I know I sound ungrateful, but it's awful and Alexis, who guzzles champagne by the gallon and owns a vinery close to Epernay, would have spat it out.

Fortunately for us British, we are able to have a great time and act civilly despite knowing that things aren't quite what they appear. I'm sure, and I can tell by the looks on our guests' faces, most present don't believe the secret agent story and are wondering just how deeply involved I was in one of the most publicised frauds of recent times. Although I haven't been put on trial, a concession to me *cooperating fully with enquiries*, and technically still working for the National Crime Agency – the NCA – I think the majority of people here think of me as being a criminal. The black sheep of the Wilson family. It provides a certain notoriety, and I'm convinced most present came because they liked the idea of rubbing shoulders with me because of my questionable claim to fame.

Just over one year ago, I fled the country with a canvas holdall stuffed full of money. One hundred thousand pounds, which had been the reward for my role in the fraud scheme that netted Alexis twenty-five million pounds. He had planned to defraud Hamlays of a lot more, one hundred million to be precise, but I got in his way, and he decided to pull the plug and leave the country. One hundred thousand sounds a lot – and it is – but if you need to live off a hundred thousand for a long time then your options are limited. And I was in a panic. Where can I go and how long can I survive on a hundred grand? But, on top, I had luckily and coincidentally come into the possession of Matlock's two hundred and fifty thousand euros, which had been his final payment for cooking Alexis's books for more than eight years. Oh, and fifty thousand pounds that had been all that was left of his illegal rewards from his dubious decade-long career as chief manipulator of financial statements. At the time, I had no idea that he was a gambler and had lost everything he owned.

On that fateful Sunday in March of last year, when I rode my scooter over to the Holden Industrial site in Horsham to collect my money, I found out that Alexis was clearing out. He was set to leave the country and to let Holden Industrial, a company he had owned for many years, and which had been the vehicle for his fraud, crash into the wall. He had no intention of telling me about his plans, and I found out quite simply because I'd been observing the old warehouse where we were set to meet for the handover. I had sneaked in and heard what they were planning. After the handover, I ran with my hundred grand stashed into a plastic bag, madly and desperately thinking through the options open to me. If I hadn't stumbled across Matlock dead in his car, I wouldn't have got far with a hundred grand. But with his stack of cash bolstering my funds, I thought I had the beginnings of a new life and therefore scarpered, nicking Uncle George's yacht from the marina in Shoreham and sailed for the Continent.

"So, you are working for the government now?"

Startled, I turn to see Ian, an old school friend, standing behind me. I turn in my chair. He kneels to be at the same level with me.

"Ian," I say. "Great to see you. How have you been doing?" Ian had been one of my best pals at school. Tall, lanky with red hair and freckles, he'd been the best soccer player and top scorer in our team. Going bald prematurely, he's lost none of his lankiness. "Spider" was his nickname.

"Fine," he replies. "So, what's this about you being a secret undercover agent, then?"

"Is that what Ben told you?" I ask, noticing that Zuki is straining to hear whilst pretending to be listening to something my mother is saying.

"Yes," says Ian nodding, "although it sounds a bit far-fetched."

"Well, I was working for the government, but that's long finished. I'm working for an investment company in Cyprus now."

"Cyprus?" he says with raised eyebrows.

"Yes, nice in Cyprus. Warm and sunny."

"Ah, well," he says, standing up, stretching his leg. "My knee," he adds by way of an explanation.

"Good to see you, Neil, and you must bring Zuki down to the pub on Friday."

"Sure," I say, although it's the last thing I plan on doing.

My thoughts return to the events of last year. After making it across the Channel, high on adrenaline and full of hope, I'd tried to live a new life but hadn't realised that life as a fugitive would be so difficult. Life on the run had very quickly become a miserable experience, and I'd given up after a few months, taking up an offer conveyed to me through Ben from the NCA. It had been simple enough: *return the money, work for us as an undercover agent and we'll do our best to get you a lesser sentence.* I agreed, so I suppose that meant I had become an undercover agent of sorts, albeit reluctantly. The agency sent over two agents to Cannes where I was living under the radar on the backpacking trail. John Williams, a burly and experienced City of London police officer, and Alice Jefferson, a forensic analyst, Jodie Foster lookalike, and a very smart and sharp lady. The plan the agents had was crazy, at least from my point of view. What they wanted was for me to infiltrate Alexis's organisation and spy on his numerous activities. But it worked, and now, here I am officially employed by Alexis and sort of married to his goddaughter.

I return my focus to the party. Zuki and I go through the motions of being the happy wedded couple, and it is with some relief when the party finally comes to an end and the guests leave with emotional goodbyes and hearty hugs. Zuki and I retire to our room, change into joggers and T-shirts, and return downstairs to help clear up and do the washing up. Washing up – that's a Wilson philosophy I explained to Zuki yesterday evening. It was her first day with the Wilson clan and she became a witness to the little quirk that glasses are always washed by hand and never in the dishwasher. A clash of culture for Zuki, who is very American when it comes to creature comforts.

Task completed, we retire to the lounge and the sofa, where I sit next to Zuki who is flicking through a celebrity magazine my mum likes buying on a regular basis, stroking the small bulge underneath the fabric of her T-shirt. I glance at the glossy photos, but in fact I'm watching Ben out of the corner of my eye. He's in the dining room, standing by the table, drinking the remainder of Pimm's and lemonade directly from the bowl. He's swaying a bit, having had too much to drink. Claire, his wife, walks into the dining room, wordlessly takes the empty bowl from him and returns to the kitchen.

I realise I haven't seen Claire all day. She's remained in the kitchen the whole time. It's quite easy to explain: Claire hates me and she's the only one here who has decided not to like Zuki. It's a jealousy thing, I think.

I can tell Ben is ready for a fight. He has been building up to this ever since we got in yesterday afternoon from the airport. It won't take long now. Five minutes later, he's ready. He comes in from the dining room, slightly unsteady.

"*Sooooo*, Neil…" he says, his voice slurring and drawing out the o's. It's Ben's preferred opener when he wants to get quarrelsome. I ignore him. "Sooooo," he says again, waiting for me to give him my attention. "Neil, what have you actually been doing since Cannes? When was that, August?"

I change my mind, deciding to engage with him as it's inevitable. "Well, Ben, as you know, I'm working as a general manager for an investment company in Limassol."

"So, not on the payroll of the government?"

"No, that chapter's closed."

"And, to whom does this investment company belong?"

I know where this is heading, and he's beginning to make my blood boil. Ben quite rightly thinks I have become part of what he calls "Alexis's gang". I sense Zuki stiffening on the sofa beside me. I have forewarned her, but this is the first time she's met Ben and so far, she hasn't experienced his annoying habit of getting on everyone's nerves. Now, less than twenty-four hours since arriving here, she's about to experience one of Ben's little outbursts.

"It belongs to the shareholders, Ben."

"And they are?"

"Ben, you're pissing me off. What are you getting at?"

"YOU!" he shouts. Mum dashes over from the kitchen, tea towel in hand and a shocked expression on her face. Claire wisely stays in the kitchen. She agrees with Ben and hates me for my involvement with Alexis and the shame I brought upon the family.

"YOU are such an arsehole, Neil. You're still up to your tricks!"

"Ben," I say as calmly as possible, "fuck off. I'm working for an investment company. It's all legitimate."

And it is. I have an employment contract to prove it and a salary. The fact that the company I am working for, Stellar Holdings, is Alexis's own private investment company doesn't need mentioning. I'm looking after legitimate businesses. And, admittedly, some not so legitimate. Ben doesn't know any of that. He doesn't know that we're running VAT scams in Europe and participating in dividend fraud schemes in Germany. And he doesn't know that top rank amongst our not so legitimate projects was a heist, which sounds nicer than robbery, last November. A cyber-attack on a bank in Germany that netted us slightly more than ten million euros. But that's not something you brag about even if it was a nice little coup. And it's certainly something that doesn't need to bother him either.

Despite my guilty conscience of committing such a crime, I am happy to have three and half million euros, which was my share, in my account – offshore, that is. I haven't touched any of it. Not yet. Not like Gilbert – the third in our little group consisting of Alexis, Gilbert and me. Gilbert is now living in the States with Zuki's sister, Sakura, also Alexis's goddaughter. Gilbert is spending quicker than Sakura can think of things she wants, and Alexis and I are worried what will happen when Gilbert runs out of money. But all that is none of Ben's business and nothing to be thinking of here and now.

"Oh no, Neil. You're a seed gone bad, that's what you are," Ben says, resuming his drunken admonition. He turns to Zuki. "You just be careful around him, Zuki. He's rotten to the core."

At that point, I come close to hitting him, but Zuki holds me back as she notices me tensing up. I can't let him speak to me like that. It's more than insulting even if it *is* true. But I can't let him get away with it especially as Mum is watching me closely. I guess she's thinking the same as Ben, but in contrast to him, she'd never say what she's thinking. And, of course, it's totally embarrassing, especially for Zuki. What Ben doesn't know is that Zuki knows all about it. She's as much a part of it as I am, even if she wasn't personally involved in that little project. Perhaps that's why Zuki stays so cool. As I say, she's good.

"Ben," she says in a voice that is soothing, like a mother speaking to an upset child. "I think you've had too much to drink. Would you like a cup of tea? I'll make one for you."

One thing Zuki has learnt from her previous visits to England is that the British solve every problem with a cuppa. And it's no different in the Wilson clan. A cup of tea will help put the world to rights.

She struggles to get up, Mum's settee being so low. Ben, now feeling ashamed, helps her up, and she rewards him with her warmest smile. It never fails. Ben goes red in the face. Taking him by the hand, she leads him out of the lounge, into the hall and through to the kitchen. Mumbling an apology, Ben trails behind like a little kid, an expression of puppy love on his face. As they walk through to the kitchen, I see Claire walk out the other side and into the dining room. She sits down with a sour face at the dining room table, puts her smartphone down on the table and flicks back and forth on the screen. I hear Zuki saying, "Now, Ben, what's troubling you?" from the kitchen. He mumbles something in a little kid's voice. Ben has never taken his drink well. God, what an idiot, I think.

In bed that night, Zuki says to me something I've never contemplated before. "He's envious," she sums Ben up. "Look at him. He's caught in his humdrum job and in his boring marriage."

Is that so? Is Ben envious of his kid brother's exploits? I doubt he's envious of the criminal aspects of my exploits, but I can imagine him being happy with three and a half million stashed away in an account somewhere. But Zuki's right in the sense that Ben seems stuck. Stuck in a life he doesn't like much and a marriage that has turned tedious. Claire is a bore, and I have never understood the attraction between the two of them. Irrespective of that aspect, Ben has always been one to lash out in order to vent his frustrations – especially when he's drunk. Zuki has good perception and insight into what triggers people. I have known Ben all my life, yet Zuki has only for slightly more than twenty-four hours. Perhaps that's all she needed to understand Ben better than I do.

Zuki falls asleep, her arm across my chest. I lie awake, listening to the gurgling in the old water pipes, the whistle of the wind rushing down the old chimney stack and the soughing of the trees as the gusts blow through the branches. If I focus, I can faintly make out the sound of the waves crashing onto the beach down the road. It must be high tide. These are the familiar sounds of my childhood. Quite suddenly, I feel a sharp prick of sadness. Sadness for leaving all this behind. Worthing, my hometown, my friends and a life entwined within this small coastal community. Mum and even Ben – the only real brother I have. Ben is six years older than me. My two other brothers are Doug, who is the eldest at twelve years older, and Will, who is ten years older. Doug and Will, we're worlds apart, and not just geographically. Doug is a lawyer in New York and Will is now a partner in a big accounting firm in Australia. Doug and Will were never close to me, and their indifference towards me, the unwanted kid brother, unwanted at least where my father was concerned, was always palpable. I can't even remember when I last spoke to them.

I lie listening to Zuki's breathing, trying to think of other things. I make the mental effort of reliving the memory of our walk into town yesterday afternoon, strolling down to the seafront, the tide out and a blue sky providing the perfect postcard backdrop. We walked along the promenade down to the pier where I bought Zuki a 99, the soft ice cream with the chocolate Flake in it. We walked along the pier, to the very end, where the anglers always stand, eating the ice cream, the wind in Zuki's hair and her eyes smiling at me. I think ahead to the week I have organised: our trip down to Devon and the ridiculously expensive hotel in Salcombe I have booked. But the memories intrude once more, and I find myself reliving the events of last year.

My involvement in the Holden Industrial fraud severed the link to my home and what's left of my family, my mum and Ben. Okay, I've only got myself to blame; it was my decision that set everything in motion. Staring into the darkness, listening to the sounds of the house and the incessant wind outside, I ask myself if I regret my actions. Has my life changed for the better or for the worse? I can't say that I want my old life back. If it hadn't been for the events of last year, I wouldn't have met Zuki and I wouldn't be leading such an addictively exhilarating life as I am now. But I acknowledge that I have been cast adrift, a stray planet in Alexis's orbit. My thoughts fix on to Alexis, a man larger than life and in some ways my mentor and my nemesis. A dominant man, admittedly like my father in many aspects. Do I regret our paths crossing and me becoming sucked into his world? That indeed is a difficult question to answer, and the only answer I can find, as my eyes become heavy and I slip into sleep, is that time will tell.

3

Alexis sits behind his old cedar desk with the faded green leather top in his study in Camiro, his magnificent house in the hills above Limassol, close, but not too close, to the village of Akrounta. His study, hidden in the recesses to the side of the main house, and formerly the pig barn so Alexis once told me, is two-thirds wood-panelled and one-third rough stone wall. Alexis calls it the "pig parlour" – a term he finds incredibly amusing. It permeates history combined with Alexis's own particular aura, giving it a warm and cosy feeling. On top, the thick panelling provides some insulation in the cold winter months. Alexis has some old wooden filing cabinets standing in here, an old-style safe and some shelves fixed to the dark wood panels, mostly taken up with framed photos of family and friends. There's one shelf dedicated exclusively to Michalis, his friend and partner of many years and Zuki's and Sakura's father. Set in the middle of the stone wall is an old steel woodstove, blackened by a century's use. Either side of the fireplace there were once small windows set into the wall, but these have been replaced by large, latticed French doors that open onto a small patio and beyond the terrace and garden with its manicured lawn, providing a view of the distant hills of the Troodos Mountains.

The setting of Camiro is so undeniably wonderful that Alexis decided many years ago to make this his central home, breathing life back into the ruins of the old farm that had been in his family's possession for God knows how long. I can't blame him; it's a wonderful house. Zuki and I have opted to spend most of our time here, rather than in the penthouse flat in the new marina development Alexis has made available to us down in Limassol, where the nightlife and the action is. The cosy and almost antique atmosphere of the study is deceptive. There are no secret documents or treasures here, those are all stored in reinforced steel cabinets down in the cellar, but this is the room Alexis inhabits and from where he manages his empire. Hidden away from view is his laptop that provides access to his international IT network. Everything here is state-of-the-art technology, and the room is constantly swept for bugs and secured by motion detectors.

Zuki and I exchange a brief look, our thoughts unspoken but heavy with the awareness of the roles we now fulfil. We have become his advisors, executives and operators since Michalis passed away last November. Alexis always says Michalis was his *numbers man*, but Michalis was more than just that. Michalis had been by his side for decades. Their lives had been intertwined from childhood onwards. A relationship forged on mutual trust and loyalty over many years.

As I sit opposite Alexis, watching him shuffling the pages with the notes he's made, preparing himself mentally to pitch his idea to us, I can't help but think here we are. Look at us. We are the new inner circle now, and once more there's that tingle of excitement at being part of the intimate core.

I steal a glance at Zuki, who is watching Alexis, too. There's a frown of concentration on her face. I can't help but feel that Zuki has always known her father was the architect behind Alexis's fortunes. She just never spent any time in her life actively thinking about it. Not until now. But the vacuum Michalis has left, I can only scratch the surface on how deep it reaches. The two built an empire encompassing so many legal and illegal operations it boggles the mind. Ever since Zuki and I became an item, and decided to stay in Cyprus, we became part of Alexis's court. Now we are summoned to fill the vacuum, no matter how deep it is, and how much of it I can grasp.

What about Zuki? Not only her relationship with Alexis, but her matching up to her father's legacy are stresses, the impact of which I can't gauge. As much as we have discussed our new duties, I don't know where her limits begin and end with Alexis. It is his universe, and he is the sun around which we revolve in our individual orbits. Will he obliterate us if we gravitate too close?

Briefly, I think back to how Zuki and I met. We fell in love on Alexis's yacht – *Axiom* – a dashing two-masted schooner whilst I was being spirited away from Cannes, a seeming plea for rescue carefully planted, and which Alexis gladly hosted. I worry what will become of Zuki, and ultimately us, the longer we are exposed to Alexis in such an intimate way. But Zuki, to my great surprise, has so far shown no qualms following in her father's footsteps. In fact, as we sit in the weighty wood-panelled study, with the responsibilities imposed upon us, I can sense the invisible hammer forging our mutual relationships anew, and stronger.

Done with shuffling papers, Alexis fixes his gaze onto his audience. "I have an interesting opportunity," Alexis says, keen to get started. His excitement is tangible, his nervous fidgeting emphasising the extent of his impatience to get started on this project. He's been chomping at the bit for days now, hurrying us to return to Cyprus despite his promise to let us enjoy what was supposedly our honeymoon. We'd been back ten minutes, just long enough to drop our bags and say hello to Isabelle, Alexis's long-suffering French wife, before he commanded us to follow him to his study. And now we sit waiting for him to reveal his latest idea.

Alexis is a big man, just under two metres tall. I have no idea how much he weighs, but his girth is as massive as his appetite. He has let his white hair grow long, wearing it in a ponytail most days. He sports a beard, well-trimmed and oiled. I smile as I look at him; I can't help but think he looks like a cross between Pavarotti and Vangelis. "Vavarotti" I call him when the kids are here, staying for the weekend, and we're playing hide-and-seek. "Find Vavarotti," I'll call out to them. He also has a love of garish coloured shirts, and when he ambles over to the pool, he looks like Father Christmas on holiday. He is quite simply the most amazing person I have ever met. Loud, gregarious, generous, incredibly astute and totally lacking in morals, especially when he's defending those dear to him.

"A very interesting opportunity indeed." He grins at us. "An opportunity to invest in a bank. An established private bank, which means family owned, with a wide portfolio of business activities," he says, leaning back in his old wooden office chair. It creaks as it strains to support the redistribution of his weight.

So far so good, I think. Sounds interesting – a potentially good investment. I nod in affirmation, waiting for more to come.

"This particular bank needs fresh capital. An indirect investment," he states. I look at Zuki. She's now frowning, puzzled by his words. I feel the same emotion stirring.

"What kind of indirect investment?" I ask. I had understood he wanted to buy into a bank, but this now sounds like a different scheme.

"The kind that is discrete," he replies. Registering our lack of comprehension, he takes a different approach. "Imagine a bank that has hit tough times – no fault of their own, I hasten to add – and is seeking fresh capital. The kind of capital injection that is discrete and not to be publicised. Capital that will steady the ship and enable the bank to continue on its promising course. Now, if the regulators were to find out they're seeking fresh capital from outside, it would mean all kinds of questions. Unnecessary trouble that," he says, waving his hand in the air. "But no capital investment means problems: more audits and investigations, perhaps in time even revocation of their banking licence. Not to mention loss of trust and confidence both from clients and the market and all that. So, looking for discrete investors, the opportunity has been disclosed to a select circle of people, including me."

A discrete investment? I think now, wondering if discrete means illegal. Alexis's legitimate and not quite so legitimate business activities merge seamlessly. "And who's approached you?" I ask, trying to understand the dimensions of this.

"A trusted friend," Alexis says.

"Like whom? Are you going to tell us or is that information too discrete?"

Alexis gives me a long look, contemplating whether he should say. In the end he gives in, sighs and drops the first bomb. "Willem."

Willem? The name is familiar, but I struggle momentarily to get my brain into gear, and then it hits me. "Willem? As in Willem de Vries?"

Alexis nods. My mouth gapes open, and Zuki looks from Alexis to me and back again.

"Who is Willem de Vries?" she asks.

"Willem de Vries happens to be a major player in the Holden Industrial fraud. He was CEO at Hamlays Bank and helped to implement the fraud scheme that…" I let my words trail off there, seeing Alexis's expression turn sour. He doesn't like any talk about Holden Industrial. Zuki looks from me back to Alexis, an intense expression on her face as the information sinks in. She connects the dots in her mind, as she knows from me all the details about the fraud and Willem's role. Alexis is watching her closely, but she keeps her face blank.

"Yes," he says after a pause, turning back to me. "Willem would invest, but he currently has other priorities and business interests. But he thought this might be something for us."

There it is – that "us". He's making it a collective thing now. *Us* ensures we are in on the decision and consequently *in* on whatever lies behind that simple term "investment".

"What's the purpose and benefit of this investment?" Zuki asks. I am no longer surprised by analytical questions like this from my wife-to-be, even if this question will rile Alexis. For somebody who has studied art and lived an unsullied life like hers, she's adapting quickly.

"The purpose?" Alexis asks, surprised that a question like that should even be asked. "Quite simply, access to a bank from the inside," Alexis replies. "The benefit? Manifold. Not just in terms of a return on investment, but plenty of business opportunities and a channel for payment streams. And a vehicle for special projects." He winks at me. I know what he means. Special projects is our term for schemes the other side of legal, and which generate cash flow and profits.

"This investment," Zuki says, but then pauses to sort out her thoughts, before continuing, "is discrete and indirect because?"

"Because we provide the capital to the family that owns the bank."

For me it's now clear. They – the family, the owners – are broke. Must be.

"Why don't you buy shares?" Zuki asks.

"Because, my dear, buying shares means visibility," Alexis explains. "And I don't want that kind of visibility. What I want is influence and, over time, some level of control. I don't need to be a shareholder to achieve that."

"And which bank is this?" I ask, still trying to work out just what potential horrors lie beneath this secret proposition. I reach for my bottle of water, taking a sip.

"An old acquaintance," Alexis says, smiling at me. "Canarus."

A spray of water erupts from my mouth. I look up at him not believing my ears. "You what?" I exclaim before whatever water is left in my mouth catches in my throat and I collapse in a fit of coughing. Even Zuki, mouth gaping, can't believe her ears.

"Canarus?" I croak after my coughing and spluttering fit ceases.

I glance across at Zuki. She's dumbstruck like me. Canarus was the German bank we robbed in November last year. A clever little operation, involving the skills of Gilbert, whom I'd befriended in Cannes the previous summer. Gilbert had inside knowledge of the workings of their software system, which we put to good use. Infiltrating their back-end software, we managed to override the system and robbed them of a day's worth of payouts in their asset finance business: ten and a half million euros was the loot. I hate to say so, but it had been my idea.

Alexis is smiling at us. "Just think about it," he says. "It's wonderful. We can use their money to fund the investment."

"How much is this proposed investment?" Zuki asks.

"Ten million minimum," Alexis replies, a devil's grin firmly in place.

"Ten million? That's handy," I say. "But the ten million is gone. You have three and a half, so does Gilbert and so do I."

"It's just money, Neil," he says. "Don't worry, I don't want you to put your share in the kitty, unless you want to." I certainly don't. And Gilbert, well, he won't either. He's enjoying life. But Alexis, well, he has plenty. I know because I work for him and have access to his accounts. All of them. And so does Zuki. He has a multitude of ten million available.

But I cringe inwardly. Morally, it's a dilemma – for me at least. I know that mentally debating the morals of doing such an investment is nonsensical if you are part of the organisation that robbed them of ten million in the first place. Robbing a bank is immoral, not to say criminal, but then investing the ten million back into them is like hitting somebody on the head only to dress the wound afterwards. But to Alexis doing one thing doesn't exclude doing the other. Quite the opposite. Our little coup has apparently weakened Canarus, and now there's an opportunity to exploit the situation and expand on it. To him it makes perfect sense. I feel miserable with guilt at the prospect.

Alexis wants to start immediately on the details, but we force him to agree to a break. A break for me and Zuki to go for a swim in Camiro's courtyard pool and to wash off the grime and dust from travelling.

***

As I lie at the far end of the pool, arms resting on the coping, I contemplate Alexis's revelations and the bombshells he has just dropped. My eyes hover over the façade of Camiro. Each brick, the lattice windows quietly radiating amongst those hard, rocklike edges, the clay tiles interwoven atop the undulating roofline, everything – new and old – seamlessly blended into perfect symbiosis and preserved, as if bathed in a vat of formaldehyde. It is all like a warm smile from an old, dependable friend.

The cool water laps over my body, and I'm struck by the realisation that here, where I now rest, there was once only earth, and the place where the farmer of old stored his tools and his meagre crop.

Antique or modern, I can't help thinking that this house is like an old watch face, a mother-of-pearl screen obscuring the cold mechanism clicking behind the scenes. These century-old bricks are only kept from bowing outward because of Alexis's money-making machine of fraud. Am I any better? Money certainly eased the outcome of my own saga with Hamlays, and here I am, increasingly fuelling

34

that same machine, making it my own. That coup, which netted us ten million, that was mine.

So why should I be surprised that he's still in touch with Willem – bomb number one. I'm forced to admit that it isn't really that surprising. But still, I'm mystified, and I still haven't worked out whether they were in cohorts about crashing Holden Industrial or not, but bomb number two, Canarus, really shocks me. I have just about come to terms with our coup and have managed in the last few months to put my guilty conscience into neutral. I have worked hard to convince myself that they must have been insured and their customers, too, so I have successfully compartmentalised my guilt until it no longer keeps me awake at night. But now, my worst nightmare has resurfaced.

Whilst unpacking and sorting through our cases and bags, we continue to process the information and busy ourselves with mundane things. "I can't believe it," I say, tossing our dirty clothes into the laundry baskets in the en suite bathroom. I sit down on the edge of the bed.

"No, neither can I," Zuki replies, busying herself with folding unused clothing and putting the garments back into the built-in wardrobe. Zuki lets out a sigh and comes to sit beside me. She takes my hand. I put her hand to my lips and kiss it. She smiles at me.

"I love you," I say. "Desperately. And truthfully, all three of those little words."

"I love you, too." She smiles at me and puts her other hand on the growing bulge of her stomach.

"We shouldn't be doing this," I say, watching her stroking her tummy.

"Doing what? Holding hands?" She laughs.

"No, I mean Alexis. And his projects. And—" I can't find the right words "—all that stuff."

She studies my face. "No," she says after a while. "But we're family. And this is what this family does."

"You serious?" I say, startled by her answer. "But a lot of it is illegal and, well, Canarus, that was criminal and immoral, and now, investing in them, that's doubly immoral."

"We were pirates to start off with. I always remember my dad telling us how the families here in Cyprus fought together for their existence. No one distinguished between right and wrong in those days because it was a fight for survival. Nothing's changed."

"But we're not fighting for survival now, Zuki. We can go and live a normal and honourable life. An honest, law-abiding life."

"Yes, of course, but this is family. It's blood, Neil. It's our history, our present and our future."

"You amaze me, Zuki, you really do."

She kisses me. "But you still love me," she adds. It's not a question but a statement.

"More than anything, my love," I say. "But it's not exactly an honourable profession, is it?"

"What isn't?"

"Being a pirate."

She laughs. "No, but an exciting one."

And that's it, end of discussion. For the time being at least. My wife-to-be does this to me frequently nowadays – shocks me into silence. She's taken to this life so easily and so quickly that it leaves me amazed and speechless. She's been totally absorbed into Alexis's world without any questioning. We sit a bit longer, holding hands and stroking Zuki's growing bulge. With a sigh and a quick kiss, Zuki rises to go to the bathroom. I remain sitting, my mind wandering back and forth contemplating what lies before us. The toll of the dinner bell, another wonderful little quirk of this family, brings my reverie to an end. My turn to sigh and go to the bathroom.

***

Alexis greets Zuki with a French-style kiss, one cheek and then the other. I get a bear hug. We only parted company a couple of hours ago, but for Alexis it's a genuine sign of affection to greet us like that.

"ManManaMan, sit down," Alexis says to me after he releases me from his hug. ManManaMan is the nickname Alexis has given me. He thinks I look like Steve McManaman, the English footballer whom Alexis admires so much.

The dining area is a vast open space set next to the large kitchen with its enormous Aga, yards of work surfaces and pots and pans hanging on hooks above the Aga. The dining table accommodates ten people easily and is the social focal point in this house. Sliding glass doors lead out onto the patio by the courtyard pool. Alexis has a separate fridge here, as tall as me, exclusively for his wine and champagne. He opens the fridge door, extracting a bottle of champagne, his standard beverage. Carafes of iced water and wine in a cooler stand on the table, and I fill my glass with water before he has a chance to pour me some champagne.

"Zuki, wine for you?" he asks.

"Alexis," Isabelle chides him. "*Mon Dieu, non. No wine for Zuki.*" Her look is stern; she shakes her head vigorously. Since Zuki announced that she's pregnant, Isabelle mothers her, which Zuki endures with stoic patience. Zuki rolls her eyes. We have this conversation almost every evening.

"Water will be fine, Alexis," Zuki says.

Most of the time Isabelle does the cooking. Sometimes even Alexis, and he's not a bad cook either. Everything Greek is his domain. It explains his girth, which has grown considerably since he left England. Heavy, over-spiced food is his specialty, which I combat with vigorous physical workouts together with Vincent. Vincent is Alexis's bodyguard, driver and handyman around the house. He's family – one of Alexis's many nephews. Vincent's real name is Dimitrios, but he gave himself the name Vincent after seeing the film *The Crimson Rivers* starring French actor Vincent Cassel. Today, the housemaid has prepared dinner: salads, grilled vegetables and chicken. We help ourselves from the dishes she's lined up.

"How was your trip?" Isabelle asks. "Did you have a nice time with your family?"

I'm quite often surprised by Isabelle. She's a small and dangerously thin woman, on the verge of being anorexic. She used to be a photo model in her younger days and judging by the photos I've seen of her, a Twiggy lookalike, albeit thirty years after such a look was fashionable. Isabelle has her blonde hair cut short giving her a boyish appearance. She appears vacant and superficial half the time, only to surprise me with firm views and perceptive insight. She urged us to go over to England in the first place. "Your poor *Maman*," she kept saying, "she must miss you so much. You are her *bébé*, her baby, *non*?!" I had decided to like her for that.

Zuki and I report on our trip to England. First our stay in Worthing and the party Ben organised for us.

We don't go into detail about that, but we have a few laughs at Ben's expense. Despite the laughs, I keep the pang of pain I felt at leaving my family behind once more to myself. Then our trip down to Devon and the wonderful little towns and villages plus the long sandy beaches we spent lazy days exploring. Alexis is quiet during dinner following our conversation but not commenting. To him, England is a country that he's crossed off on his list. Despite his many years in England, he has shut that chapter for good, saying that England never brought him any luck. But Zuki and I know why he's quiet. He's waiting to get back to business. Isabelle never allows talk of business during dinner, but come coffee and liqueurs there's no holding him back.

"So, what do you think about that investment?" he asks, no longer being able to wait. Isabelle groans and gets up to clear the dishes.

"You've already made up your mind, Alexis," I say, refilling my glass, my eyes on him. "Any more bombs you want to drop? Before I take a sip?"

Alexis laughs. "No, my friend, no more bombs."

"I have no experience of things like this, but if you're going to invest discretely, then how are you going to secure your investment?" I ask. "Apart from the obvious of setting up a contract, of course, and some collateral that they might offer."

"Quite right. Now you're beginning to think like a real businessman. A contract, of course that's a necessity. But securing our investment as you say is tricky when the structure is like this. Think on it, Neil, see what you come up with."

I should be able to hear the warning bells by now, but I don't. Zuki does, and she gives Alexis a long, beseeching look, which he ignores.

"There's only one thing to do," I carry on, seeing the exchange of looks between Zuki and Alexis but not realising the meaning and riding myself deeper into the mire. "Meet with them. Discuss the offer and then find the appropriate solution."

Alexis nods. "Exactly, Neil. Exactly. We fly tomorrow."

4

"Neil, I'm not sure about this venture and this country," Alexis says out of the blue.

"Bit late now," I reply, turning to face him.

"Well, I have this phobia about German sausages," he says.

"What?"

"I fear the *wurst*," he says, no longer being able to hold back his laughter.

From the front Vincent joins in, although I doubt he knows what *wurst* means. It's a pathetic joke and a silly play on words, but okay, humorous. I smile.

Vincent drives the big black Mercedes hire car onto the exit lane of the airport, easing the car into the stream of traffic on the motorway. Whilst he gently accelerates the big car to match the flow, I resume my position gazing out of the window. Through the black-tinted glass everything looks grey and drab, despite the sun shining. Far away on my right, I spot the tall radio and television tower that stands over two hundred metres tall right in the centre of town.

Düsseldorf: I've been here before but don't have many memories of it. I remember the old town, the

Altstadt, and the pubs lined up one next to the other. *Die längste Theke der Welt*, the longest bar in the world, the locals are reported to say with pride. But then it could just be a clever marketing thing. Well, we'll have a chance to explore that this evening, as we have booked a hotel for the night before flying back to Cyprus tomorrow.

Düsseldorf is where Canarus has its head office. The full name is *Bankhaus August Canarus AG*. A private bank, established in Belgium in the eighteenth century before the tides of history and fortune left what remained of it after two world wars in Düsseldorf. Here it prospered, especially after the Second World War, and the *Wirtschaftswunder*, the miraculous economic recovery, and became an established bank serving its German customer base.

From my previous research, I know it's been in the ownership of the Borrell family for over a hundred years. Despite my dread of coming here, and the totally unlikely chance of meeting Kerstin, the employee at Canarus we had groomed for our digital hit-and-run, and who'd inadvertently set everything off, I now feel a weird sense of excited expectation.

We're on our way, sitting in the sleek black Mercedes with Vincent acting as chauffeur, to have that meeting with the Borrells. In a way it feels like returning to the scene of crime, as often depicted in movies, except I never set foot here to execute the crime. The coup we carried off had been performed from a safe distance. A cyber-attack, a digital hit-and-run, more akin to a video or computer game and which at the time did not feel *real*. But the impact had been real enough, and now we're going to meet the real flesh-and-blood people on whom we inflicted this damage. If Alexis feels any unease, he doesn't show it. I doubt he feels anything – except the thrill of the hunt.

We sit in silence, Vincent driving, and Alexis and I absorbed in whatever thoughts are running through our minds. I look out of the tinted side window, the verges and banks of the motorway a blur, and beyond these the uniform modern glass and concrete offices and industrial buildings that probably line every airport motorway around the world. After twenty minutes, Vincent takes the car onto another motorway heading south towards Cologne, and sooner than expected we exit from the motorway, turning onto an A-road and follow the route on the sat nav that takes us up into a hilly area. A sign flashes past, something with *Neanderthal*, but I can't read it in its entirety.

"How appropriate," Alexis comments and smiles at me. "Going to meet the Neanderthals."

I could tell him that this is a historic site, the Neander Valley, where a century ago archaeologists found remains of an ancient Neanderthal tribe, but things like that are of no interest to Alexis. To him there's only one historic culture of any significance, namely the Greek. We drive on, trees and hedges lining the road. Occasionally, gaps appear allowing brief glimpses of the big houses tucked away behind them. Quite unexpectedly, the trees open up, a golf course appearing on the right and allowing us to briefly watch golfers in gaudy trousers and polo shirts going about their serious sport. The car park is full of big cars: Mercedes, BMWs, Porsches and Maseratis. Alexis lets out a soft whistle. "Rich pickings," his sanguine comment.

Driving on, the trees and high hedges reclaim their prominent position bordering the road. The houses behind them now seemingly even bigger and grander. Vincent slows, focussing on the sat nav display, and flicks on the indicator at the last moment, turning onto the gravel driveway of a large villa. As the car crunches along, I get to view the house. It's grand and old, at a guess I'd say built over two hundred years ago in that solid neo-classical style that was the favourite of the rich at the time. The imposing house is flanked by two flat-roofed annexes, one each side of the three-storeyed main house. Thick columns support the roof of the porch on the main house, and above that another two floors rise up with tall windows topped with window crowns and a dominant roof. On the wall just below the roof, I can make out an inscription in gold lettering: *audentes Fortuna iuvat*. I read the inscription but have no idea what it means. Flanking the main house on both sides, the two flat-roofed annexes, perhaps additions from later years, box the main house in like guardhouses, giving it a stately appearance.

Vincent stops the car in front of the porticoed colonnade, worn stone steps rising up to the entrance. We get out, stretch our legs and I spot Alexis reading the inscription. "Fortune favours the bold," he says, shrugging and smiling at me. "We'll see," he adds, with a wink.

The large double front doors open and a silver-haired, well-groomed man of medium height in his sixties walks out. His smile is friendly and welcoming as he comes skipping down the steps to greet us.

"Herr Theophilou, *willkommen* – welcome," he exclaims as he walks up to Alexis.

"Alexis suffices," he replies. "Please, just call me Alexis." They both shake hands as if they've known each other for years. Alexis, I have to hand it to him, can switch on the charm at the flick of a switch. I resume my study of the smaller man, whom I have instantly recognised as being Gunter Borrell, head of the bank and head of the Borrell family. I remember from my research prior to our ploy last November that Gunter is a widower and has two sons, Ralph and Oliver.

He turns to me. "And you must be Herr—" he hesitates a second before he gets it out "—Epica." He makes it sound like a question. I just knew the name would be a hindrance wherever I go. I'll have to talk to Alexis to amend that, I say to myself as I shake his warm, manicured hand.

"Jordan," I say. "Just call me Jordan."

Gunter smiles as he releases my hand, but his smile is less enthusiastic where I'm concerned. And as he begins to turn back towards Alexis, I catch Alexis grinning at me. The sod is enjoying himself at my expense.

After beckoning us to come into the house, Gunter leads the way up the steps onto the porch and through the main doors into the house. The hall is straight out of a museum: gold-coloured wallpaper with motives of African wildlife and domestic deer and boar. Heavy antique furniture stands on the highly polished but worn wood flooring. Fancy gold and red ornaments, vases and brass candlesticks stand on top of the furniture and more brass candle holders are mounted on the walls. An enormous brass candelabra hangs from the ceiling, and I step to the side not to have to walk beneath it. The windows are covered with heavy lace curtains and thick satin drapes pulled aside and secured by tiebacks.

Gunter beams as he sees us taking in the oppressive décor. "All authentic of the time period," he says proudly. I wonder what time period he's referring to and whether the rest of the house looks the same. If it's anything like this, then to me it would be unbearable. We just nod in false exaggerated appreciation.

He then turns to the right, gesturing all the time for us to follow, like an impatient usher in a theatre, and marches us through a door which is standing open. We are now in the annex on the right-hand side of the main house. I'm struck by the change in atmosphere. Here, light colours dominate, and the first impression is, well, modern. Modern in contrast to the hall we have just passed through that is. But it's modern in an odd way, and it takes me a moment to grasp what my eyes are seeing. It's an *old* modern, in the sense of worn. Lived in, and perhaps *comfortable*, I guess one could call it. He walks over towards a large fireplace with a marble surround set in the middle of the outer wall and the focal point of the room. In front of the fireplace three two-seater sofas covered in a rich fabric are arranged with a large glass and chrome low coffee table standing in the middle.

"Please do sit," he says to us whilst looking across and behind our backs, saying something in German. I almost jump as I turn and see an elderly, hard-faced woman in old-fashioned housemaid's garb standing rigid in the corner of the room.

"*Kaffee*," he commands. The hard-faced woman nods, turns and opens a panel in the wall. She disappears through the panel, which closes with a soft click behind her. Nice, I think, a secret passageway.

Gunter launches into casual chat, asking the obligatory questions. "Did you have a good flight? Are you staying overnight? Oh, then you must visit the Altstadt. It boasts the longest bar in the world."

The door to the annex swings open and in walks a thickset young man, early thirties, I'd say, and easily recognisable as one of Gunter's sons. He looks the spitting image of his father. Equally smartly dressed, hair perfectly set but a fuller face and much fuller figure. He smiles at us, and Gunter introduces him as his younger son, Oliver. He shakes our hands, a warm pleasant smile on his face, and sits down on the sofa next to his father.

"Wo ist Ralph?" I hear his father ask. *Where's Ralph?* Oliver just shrugs.

The unsmiling housemaid reappears shuffling along slowly, carrying a tray laden with a heavy silver coffee pot and bone china cups and saucers. They look antique, and I don't fancy handling these, clumsy oaf that I am. The housemaid pours, taking her time, the conversation stopping and the silence becoming heavy as we wait for her to complete her laborious task. I can see Gunter beginning to get uncomfortable, and I wonder what he's like when in a temper. Finally finished, the housemaid turns, ignoring the glare from her master, and exits, letting the door to the annex crash loudly behind her. Gunter grimaces before smiling apologetically at us. We go through the motions of pouring milk, adding sugar, stirring and picking up the dainty cups as the door to the annex crashes open once more and bounding in come two large black doberman dogs. I freeze, cup raised halfway, as one of the dogs circles around the sofa to where I'm sitting, puts its front paws up on the cushion and sniffs my face. I like dogs, but a doberman appearing out of nowhere, and its snout and black eyes so close to your face you can smell its breath, well, it triggers some baser survival instinct. I sit frozen stiff, not daring to move, especially as it is now fixing me with a look that's turning slightly unfriendly.

I'm mesmerised by this unexpected canine intrusion. Whose dogs are these? And who let them loose on us? I'm paralysed by a growing fear and with a conscious effort, I avert my eyes from the dog's, hoping it will appease him. All I can hear is the other dog running around, apparently wagging its tail, and panting. It takes a moment for the shock to dissipate, and then I hear Gunter exclaiming and saying some choice words to someone who must be standing behind me. Whoever this is lets out a mocking laugh and calls the dog: "Hasso!"

Hasso, I now know its name, drops down from the sofa, turns and disappears. Into the space now vacated by the dog walks a man dressed in black jeans and a black shirt. I slowly put the cup down and look up to see a man slightly older than me. Dark eyes, black hair. Mid-thirties, would be my guess.

I rise, and we face each other. The man grins at me – insolently, arrogantly, daring me. He's thin and a bit taller than me. Handsome, I admit, in a dark and brooding way. He's everything his brother isn't. And, judging by the grin, he enjoyed my discomfort. I can't help but think this one's a psychopath. He introduces himself as Ralph Borrell. He reaches out to shake my hand whilst I'm still thinking how much I'd like to hit him for pulling off that little stunt. A doberman right up close in your face is not something you expect on a first visit unless you're visiting Putin. His grip is firm, very firm, and the opposite of polite. I hold my ground, applying as much pressure as he is. I can feel his ring beginning to dig into my finger.

"Jordan Epica," I say.

"Epica? An unusual name if you allow me to say so," he replies in perfect English. He releases my hand and turns to face Alexis. "And you are Mr Theophilou. I am Ralph."

Alexis, I now see, has been sitting there frozen stiff just like me. He's just about recovered his composure, sets his cup down with a trembling hand onto the table and stands to shake the young man's hand. I know he has a tremendous fear of all dogs bigger than a corgi. If it had been him coming face to face with a doberman, he'd either have screamed and

51

ran from the room, with the doberman in hot pursuit, or otherwise he'd have fainted, which is more likely.

They shake hands, but I can tell Alexis is reserved. No display of his typical jovial bonhomie, and he makes no attempt to smile that big winning smile he usually puts on. He senses the cold ruthlessness in the young man, too.

I become aware that Gunter is apologising and chiding his son for letting out the dogs at the same time. Ralph ignores him. As I watch him, the difference between the two sons becomes manifest: Ralph takes after the mother. I remember seeing photos of her when we did the research on Canarus last year. She was a keen sportswoman with a hard, ambitious face. She excelled at many sports, so it was reported. Tennis, horse riding and, if I remember rightly, she was a terrific shot. I came across photos of her posted on the website of a tennis club where she'd been an active member. I remember reading that she had won many a tournament. There was also a commentary, and it implied that her ambition matched her temperament. I deduced at the time that in between the lines, the commentary was hinting that she was egocentric. As I look at Ralph, I can't help but think that she's passed this on to her elder son, so it would appear.

Ralph turns away from Alexis and towards the sofa on which his father and brother sit side by side. Ralph has his back to me, so I can't see the exchange of looks, but I can see his brother Oliver looking up at him. An unspoken command lets him rise, and he makes space for his older brother. Ralph sits down, next to his father, leans back into the cushions and casually puts one leg over the other, boldly studying Alexis and me in turn. Gunter resumes control, focussing on Alexis.

"We are so pleased you have come to visit us. Let me explain the circumstances," he says, all business now. "We have invited you here as we think this kind of meeting is not suited for the bank's premises. It is a delicate and private matter." Alexis nods; he understands discretion. "You are perhaps aware of our recent misfortune. In November last year, we were targeted by a hostile third party, who overcame our IT system's built-in defences and managed to manipulate our back-end system in our asset finance division. These criminals managed to override our software, redirecting the payments scheduled for payout on that particular day. The fourth quarter is a busy time of the year, as you can imagine. Leading up to year end, our asset finance business is always extremely busy.

"Unfortunately, the culprits had detailed inside knowledge, and they were able to take advantage of a bug in the software that we didn't even know existed. They stole a complete day's business volume – roughly ten million euros." He pauses, looking at Alexis and me in turn, and we both nod and make appropriate noises. Of course, we know all about it, and it is with a conscious effort that I manage to keep my face straight and expression blank.

Alexis sits listening, his face a mask, sipping his coffee. Gunter looks from Alexis to me and back again. One final nod, confirming that we are aware of the events, and Gunter looks down at the table. It seems to be an emotional moment for him, which he disguises by pouring himself another coffee.

In fact, Alexis and I discussed our approach in detail prior to coming here. "We must give nothing away by our reactions," Alexis had said, knowing that I am less cool than he is. Bloody hell, sitting here, facing Gunter, my heart is thumping away inside my chest. I hope and pray it's not noticeable.

"As you can imagine, an event like that is a shock," Gunter says, resuming his tale. "A shock to us, but also to the whole banking market here in Germany. The clear-up operation took some months. First the police, then the regulators from the European Central Bank and the Bundesbank – you know, the federal state bank – our auditors, and a lot more that came and investigated the event. We are a regulated bank, but we're family owned and our resources are limited. For a short while I feared our licence might be in jeopardy. We found out that the malware, a term I'd never really been aware of prior to that day, had been infiltrated in the form of attachments to emails that an employee in the bank had received and opened. From there, the malware was able to work its way through our system and basically replace the payment instructions in the files that we send over for clearing. We tried to follow the payment stream, but we only got as far as a Russian bank, and from there the trail dissipated into thin air. Overseas accounts in God knows where. Not a chance to recover anything, and the Russian bank deny all knowledge."

Alexis and I sit and listen and make what we hope are the right sympathetic noises. I just about succeed in keeping a firm grasp on myself, as I come close to losing it, suppressing my mad urge to laugh. We know exactly where the money went. I distract myself by wondering what fate Kerstin met, and that's enough to keep me focussed. Looking at Ralph and his stupid fixed smile, I wonder if he dropped her into the Rhine with concrete shoes attached to her feet. I wouldn't put it past him.

"Good lord," Alexis says. "Incredible."

I find it incredible that he actually dares to comment on it.

"Fortunately, we are insured for such matters, so the collateral damage was limited," he says. I am grateful to hear that. "Nonetheless, the damage to our reputation cannot be underestimated," Gunter adds. "And a loss of such magnitude has left us under some strain."

Gunter turns to Oliver, who is perched on a stool by the highly polished walnut bar in the corner. "Would you be so kind to get Martha to bring us some more coffee and water?" Oliver nods, rises and walks out, the door closing behind him with a soft click. Ralph, I notice, is sitting totally at ease on the sofa next to his father, and scrutinising Alexis and me. An odd look is playing on his face, but I choose to ignore him and return my focus to Gunter.

"Gentlemen," he says in a heavy voice, "the bank regulators are looking for us to inject fresh capital. Not that we need it – our balance sheet is strong – but they want us to demonstrate our commitment."

Oliver returns, nods to his father and resumes his place by the bar.

"It is a delicate matter," Gunter continues, "for whilst we have capital reserves, these are not liquid funds." Even though his English is very good, I can sense he's struggling to find the right words. "These reserves are tied up in long-term investments, and we need time to free them up first. And, preferably not at a loss," he adds with a sigh. "Accordingly, we are inviting close associates to provide loans to tide us over. We would not approach—" Gunter struggles to find the right term "—*outsiders*, like you, my esteemed friend, to invest, but our mutual friend Willem de Vries suggested you might well be the right person to speak to."

He looks at Alexis, who has been listening with a fixed look in his eyes. Alexis makes a show of contemplation, stroking his beard in the process. He nods in affirmation, confirming that indeed he is the right person to speak to.

"What level of funding are you seeking?" Alexis asks.

Gunter swallows hard, and I can see this is hard for him. Unless he's a good actor, which I wouldn't put past him either.

"In total we are looking for fifty million euros," Gunter replies.

Fifty million? That takes me by surprise. The talk was of ten million. Alexis remains unperturbed.

"Fifty million in total," Gunter says. "Ten million per slot." He frowns. "Is that the right term? I'm not sure."

Alexis looks at me, but I'm not sure either. He turns back to Gunter. "Fifty million in total split into five ten-million loans," he says. "That's clear enough for me."

"Yes," Gunter replies. "That's the nature of it. Of course, we are happy to find other solutions if you say wanted to invest fifteen or twenty-five even. We have packaged the loans based on tenure, or is 'term' the right word? You know, three years, four or five, as you like. And the interest we are offering depending on the term. Coupled with the collateral we can offer."

"Which is?" Alexis asks.

Gunter looks in my direction. Alexis catches the meaning of that look. "Jordan is my son-in-law, my associate and has my full trust," he says. *Son-in-law?* Mentally, I'm raising my eyebrows in amused wonder but maintain my blank expression.

"Of course," Gunter concedes. "Well, we have put together collateral in the form of shares and other securities and my personal guarantee."

Alexis puts on his most earnest expression and nods his understanding. "And the interest rate?"

"Depending on tenure – or term," Gunter replies. "Base rate plus interest rate, again depending on term. The longer the loan is granted to us, the higher the interest rate will be."

"And these loans are absolutely off the balance sheet of the bank?" Alexis asks.

"Yes, by necessity." Gunter smiles, acknowledging that he thoroughly understands what Alexis wants to know.

Martha reappears, this time pushing an old-fashioned tea trolley laden with more coffee, water and various snacks and rolls. Gunter appears pleased for the interruption, and I can't say that I don't feel for him. I don't think he's acting anymore. He looks worn out, emotionally drained. It certainly must be awful for him to have to pitch for support in this way. After all, we are total strangers to him. Gunter fusses over pouring coffee and water and distributing the snacks. Oliver rushes over to help. Ralph, however, remains where he is, leaning back, legs crossed and twiddling his signet ring. I'm amazed that he is seemingly so detached from his father's predicament and the plea for help. In fact, he's looking at me, a sly smile on his lips, and I wonder just what is going on in his mind. I catch a glimpse of his signet ring – large, gold with a black face and gold letters. No wonder my fingers were getting bruised. I try to make out the letters. Difficult from my position, but I can make out an R and a B…and something else, perhaps a D? I notice Gunter is wearing an identical one, but I can't see the letters on his.

"Coffee, Jordan?" Oliver asks, bringing me out of my reverie. I take the proffered cup and notice he isn't wearing a ring.

***

"A most interesting house," I say as I stand by the tall window, with its view of the front garden and drive, the black Mercedes parked just outside. I take a sip of water from my glass, looking out over the front lawn. Oliver is standing beside me eating a sandwich.

"Yes, it has a long history," he replies, chewing and swallowing. "Built in eighteen hundred by a wealthy colonial trader. Is that the right terminology? You know, a tradesman to the colonies in Africa."

"I think we say colonial merchant," I say, not sure myself.

"It came into our possession a hundred years ago," a voice says behind me. I turn to find Ralph standing behind us.

"Certainly, a jewel in one's possessions," I say.

"Quite," he replies. "And it shall stay that way."

Oliver makes some mumbled apology and moves over to the table to refill his coffee, no doubt glad to get away from his brother. Unfortunately, I'm left standing next to Ralph.

"You see to me," he says, moving forward to stand alongside me, "this is our bastion. Our family has worked hard to build its fortune. *Audentes Fortuna iuvat.* I'm sure you saw the inscription."

"Fortune favours the bold," I echo Alexis.

"You are a student of the classics?" he asks with a note of condescending surprise. He raises his coffee cup to take a sip, and I manage to get a good look at his signet ring: RBD.

"No, can't say that I am, but some things one does pick up along the way." Again, I can sense the arrogance beneath the surface, and I can't help but feel like I want to punch him. Hard.

"I have spent a lot of time studying these things and the history of our ancestors. And we have some illustrious forebears," he adds, leaving me to wonder where this is going. "Bold men who took action rather than sit and wait for whatever fate had in store for them."

"Is that so?" I say, wishing I could get away from him.

"Did you know we are related, albeit distantly, to the flying ace Jochen Deselaers. He flew with Baron von Richthofen, of World War One fame."

"Really?" I say, not caring one bit for their illustrious forebears.

"Yes, and sometimes I wish I had been alive in those days. Gallant men who fought man to man in the skies above France. And if I could get my hands on the man who pulled off that ploy on us last November, I'd face him man to man. To the end. Just like the baron did."

Bloody hell, the guy is a nutter, I think. But deep inside me alarm bells are ringing. Is this just conversation or is there something else, something sinister to it? For a moment I wonder if somehow he knows. It might explain his constant scrutiny of Alexis and me. But I don't find the time to explore that notion, for I hear voices and turn to see Gunter and Alexis walking in through the door. Gunter has his hand on Alexis's shoulder and they seem to be laughing at some comment. I hadn't even noticed that they had left the room, so engrossed had I been in my conversation with Oliver and then Ralph. Alexis beckons to me, and I'm glad to get away from Ralph. I move over to him.

"I think we are ready to leave," he says to me.

Thank God for that, I think, but I just nod my okay.

Turning to Gunter, Alexis says, "Thank you, Gunter. We will consider this in detail but as I said, I think we can support you. We will be in touch shortly."

Gunter holds out his hand and shakes Alexis's keenly. "Many thanks for your time, my dear Alexis."

I think we can support you. My mind lingers on that sentence. I've missed out on something here, but it's not the time to ask now. Gunter escorts us to the front door where Vincent is waiting in the car. He jumps out, opens the rear door for Alexis, who climbs inside. I walk around the back, open the other rear passenger door and make to get in. I cast one last glance over to where Gunter is standing and behind him Ralph. Whilst Gunter is all smiles and waving goodbye to Alexis, Ralph has his eyes on me. Unsmiling, his expression is combative. Perhaps it's just my imagination, but it seems to me that he's looking down the sights of his machine guns.

5

Inside the cocoon of the big Mercedes, and as Vincent pulls away from the house, I feel myself relax. Through the darkened windows I look back and watch as Gunter climbs the steps to the house, passing his son Ralph without a look or even an exchange of words. Ralph stands watching us leave and only turns to go back inside when we reach the road. I wonder what that says about the relationship between father and son. A meeting of that nature and you don't say a word to each other when your guests drive off? Wouldn't it be normal to stop and say something like: *"What do you think?"* or *"That went well"*. Very strange indeed and it probably speaks volumes of the relationship between the two, but ultimately, I conclude thankfully, it's none of my concern. I'm just glad to get away.

"Jeez, that was a creepy fellow, that Ralph," I say as I lean back in my seat, relief spreading through me now the meeting is over and I can relax.

"Absolutely," Alexis says, busying himself with a small device he's holding in his hand. It looks like one of those old MP3 players to me. "A right nasty one that one, letting those two dogs loose on us."

"Too bloody right," I agree. "That doberman had foul breath."

I wonder if Alexis got what he wanted. It sounded like it, judging by that last comment: *I think we can support you*. But he's too busy fiddling around with the small device, so I don't ask. I look out of the window, letting the impressions of the meeting sink in.

"Right, sorted," Alexis says, and I turn to see what he's doing. He has attached a pair of small plug-in earphones to the device and is listening. "Excellent, all recorded and in good quality too," he says with a note of pride in his voice. He takes the plug out of his ear and turns to me. "So, what do you think?"

"I was going to ask you the same," I say.

"You go first, Neil."

"Well, Gunter seems genuine. And I had the impression he was being honest and truthful. A difficult topic to broach to strangers and at the same time, I'm sure it was painful for him to have to pitch to us. Oliver, nice enough but seemed overwhelmed by it all. And as for Ralph, well, he gave the impression of being totally bored and not wanting to be part of the whole thing. But dominant and Oliver fears him. Which makes me wonder why Gunter had both sons there…" I say, my words trailing off as I think about it. "Of course, they are shareholders," I say once I've thought it through. "So, they have to be in on any deal that is arranged." I glimpse Alexis nodding out of the corner of my eye.

"As for the deal," I carry on. "There wasn't much beef to it, was there? Of course, the event last November—" I hesitate for a moment, preferring to refer to our robbery in general terms now that I've met the Borrells "—had its effect, and I can see that the federal state bank and the ECB would be wanting the family to inject additional capital to strengthen the bank and, chiefly, to steady the nerves of the market." And whilst I'm saying this something else bubbles up: "I'm no expert on these things, but somehow, I wondered a bit about the pitch too, you know. And I know it's not the same thing, but at Hamlays everything was presented based on a proposal with reports and charts and accompanying documents. Projections for the future, the bank's underlying stability, capital strength, business development and how they expect to repay the investment. None of that here. All just words and a promise of good interest. All a bit vague."

"That's why I make use of devices like this," Alexis says, holding up the gadget. "It's a digital recorder."

"Good idea to bring that, even if not quite above board," I say. "And what struck me too," I add, "is that fifty million is a big step up from ten million. That came as bit of a surprise to me."

"Not quite so for me," Alexis says, his face turned away from me, looking out of the window. "I expected their requirement to be significantly higher than ten million. And that's because it isn't just the capital injection to fulfil the expectations from the central bank or the market. I'd say it's because they have something else to cover up."

"You what?" I ask, completely surprised by his statement. But then again, I remember my first impression when Alexis outlined the potential investment and that they were broke.

"Yes, my friend, I can tell rogues a mile off. And those three gentlemen are rogues just like us." He turns to me and smiles. "Would you trust rogues like us?"

"You're asking me? I trusted you once, remember."

Alexis laughs. "That's because at that time you were a bloody amateur, my friend. But not anymore. And these guys are professional rogues just like us."

I mull over his words in my head. I can see what he means. "So, it's off?"

"No," he replies with force. "Why should it be off? Often enough investments in schemes like this are the best investments. Sometimes, admittedly, they're not, so one has to tread carefully."

"How do you tread carefully when it's an investment like this?"

"Oh, you don't believe the projections they didn't have, as you rightly point out. You send someone to do a thorough check," he says, smiling at me, knowing full well that he's the cat that gets to enjoy the cream, and not me.

***

It isn't until later that evening, whilst over dinner in a Japanese restaurant, that Alexis reveals his real plan. By that time, I've had a few altbiers, the traditional caramel-coloured beer that is brewed in Düsseldorf, and my guard is down. We started the evening off by walking around the Altstadt, trying the various brands of altbiers brewed by the multitude of microbreweries located within a square mile radius of the old town. Germans like to drink their beer out in the open, and in Düsseldorf it's an established custom to do so standing up. Tall trestle tables stand outside the breweries and pubs, where the guests gather in groups, standing and chatting.

Alexis was a fair sport for a while, I'll give him that much. He tried a couple, saying they were okay but too bitter and not really his taste. Vincent was fine; he's a beer man. Alexis, however, guzzles champagne. It's his *aqua vitae*, his life water, so he claims. Champagne is something you won't find in an altbiers brewery in the old town of Düsseldorf and so, after a while, we left the altbiers route through the old town and went in search of food and other drinks, namely champagne.

Alexis got interested when I told him that Düsseldorf has the third largest Japanese community in Europe. On his insistence, I asked a passer-by in my rusty but otherwise good German if there was a central location in downtown Düsseldorf where one can find Japanese restaurants. We were pointed in the direction of the Immermannstraße where we would be able to find several. And this is where we are now, sitting in an authentic Japanese restaurant.

The authenticity extends so far as to providing menus in Japanese, and that means Japanese only. No English or German menus exist, but things like that never bother Alexis and certainly don't stop him.

As soon as we walked in, he put on his all-embracing smile exuding charm, and his bonhomie just sparkles into life. The Japanese staff were mesmerised from the moment he pushed open the door to the restaurant. This big man, and it's something that never ceases to amaze me, will simply take over by the sheer force of his personality.

After being seated, a couple of waiters appeared at our table, I think mainly to stare at Alexis. Not the friendliest types at the best of times, but Alexis ignored them and got the head waiter to come over and impressed him with a volley of Japanese names for the dishes. The head waiter soon realised the potential revenue he could expect and got his team working. Alexis ordered champagne, which brought a big smile to the head waiter's lips. Alexis is a serious and professional gourmand. Not surprising considering it's his favourite occupation and he owns a string of restaurants. I smile as we sit at the table, Vincent and I watching Alexis letting off volley after volley of orders, remembering when we met in August last year, in a restaurant on the beach by one of the big marinas in Cannes, and it turned out to be his restaurant that we had dined in.

As soon as the first dishes start appearing, Alexis switches into restaurant reviewer mode, which is something he enjoys doing just to scare the staff. Tucking in, he pretends to make notes on his smartphone, telling Vincent and me to do so, too. Halfway through the meal I catch a glimpse of one of the younger waiters slipping out of the door and returning soon after with a carrier bag full of champagne bottles to replenish the stock Alexis is steadily demolishing.

"That's how you do it, Neil," he says, his head turning to me, chopsticks high in the air. "And you should have picked up some of the names of these dishes from Zuki by now."

He's right. Zuki is of Japanese American descent, and she has spent thousands of hours studying the language, the history and the customs of Japan. On our first proper night out together, she found a Japanese restaurant by chance in Cagliari on

Sardinia. Taking me by the hand, she led me inside, and I remember how the proprietor came to life once Zuki started speaking to him in Japanese. He was so impressed and delighted that he went off to create some of the best food I've ever eaten. But I must add, it was Zuki who made that evening so special. Totally inept at eating with chopsticks, or *hashi* as they are called in Japanese, so Zuki informed me, she took to feeding me, selecting morsels from the various dishes and gently sliding them into my mouth. It was so sensual and erotic that I for once was grateful rather than frustrated by one of my many ineptitudes.

"I'll get her to give me some lessons when we get back," I promise.

"Start learning Greek whilst you're at it," he says. His tone is serious and he's become somewhat contentious, no doubt triggered by the amount of champagne he's knocked back. "Zuki can teach you Greek too," he adds, pointing his chopsticks at me, which is another of his favourite topics.

"Okay," I say, hoping he'll switch the subject soon. He's right, I should be making more of an effort to learn Greek to start off with and then maybe Japanese, but everyone in Cyprus is so happy speaking English to me. Plus, I'm not as gifted in learning languages like Zuki. But as in any competition, and with Alexis most things are a competition, I try to score a point. "But my German is good," I counter. And my German *is* good, in principle. German A level and some time spent here during uni days.

"Glad to hear so," he says, picking up a meat ball and eyeing it with some suspicion before popping it into his mouth. "You're going to need it," he adds whilst chewing it.

I recall him saying in the car that he wants a thorough check performed, and I assume he means that. "Sure, no problem," I say, not understanding once more what I'm getting myself into. "Should be sufficient for an audit, if that's what you want to do."

"Good, glad to hear your German's good enough," he replies. "Pass me that dish," he says to Vincent. "It certainly will improve over time whilst you are working at Canarus." He lifts out some noodles with his chopsticks and onto his plate.

"You what?" I ask, putting down my fork. Vincent and I are the only customers eating with forks, and we had to request them specifically and emphatically. Authentic Japanese restaurants don't provide forks.

"It's a precondition, I told Gunter, and he agreed," Alexis continues, as if it's just some routine conversation we're having.

"Alexis, I'm not getting what you're saying. What's this about a precondition? Can you be a bit more specific?"

He stops, noodles clamped between his hashi, his hand halfway to his mouth, eyeing me as if I've said something very curious. Frowning, he says, "But, Neil, I thought it was clear. You asked and as I said, with a deal like this there is no collateral you can really rely on except your own man inside the organisation. You will be working in a permanent capacity at Canarus. You'll be my man in the bank." I sink into my seat. My mind fogs over and my thought processes disengage with the information just received.

Far from adhering to a conscious set of instructions, like the steps you take when breaking down a puzzle, I feel my thoughts in this moment disintegrate into rippling lights, smoke dashed by rising and falling sparks, and you might as well throw in a few smashed-up mirrors too. In response to this little piece of information, embers flit across my brain, fluttering from sparks, from explosions. Each little fragment of anger reflected in the shards of mirrored glass, and magnified, and repeated over and over again as a fire erupts deep within me, not unlike the bonfire on Guy Fawkes Night in London, and takes control of my body.

"You are not serious," I say, emphasising each individual word. Vincent stops eating, eyes latching onto me. Alexis puts down his chopsticks, leans back, an exaggerated look of surprise on his face. Oh, he's such a shit actor, I think.

"I am," he replies. His eyes are fixed on me, and he can tell I'm not joking about it. He's right, for in fact now I'm boiling inside. He drops the habitual play of innocent bewilderment he puts on when he pretends not to understand. It's plainly obvious to both of us: two little words but one hundred per cent powerplay. And through the sparks in my head, and the mist of red anger that's bubbling up like lava inside me, a little part of my mind is still actually thinking – it's telling me that this is a test. A big test. A test of my loyalty. My loyalty to him and my loyalty to the family I desire to be a part of. It's an echo of what Zuki said just a day ago: *Yes, of course, but this is family. It's blood, Neil. It's our history, our present and our future.* Oh fuck, I think.

"And what do I tell Zuki?" I say.

I see in his eyes there's the slow perception of an aspect he'd forgotten about. His look crumples and his expression becomes one of confused shame. "Oh shit," he mumbles.

"Not until the baby is safely delivered," I say, knowing full well it will be even worse to leave after the child is born. "Audit, okay…but not until then will I go to work at Canarus."

"No, of course," he says, and I can tell he's trying to work out how much longer Zuki has. He's made his plans and wants them executed. And that means me going to spend a considerable time working in whatever capacity he thinks suitable within Canarus.

"Fuck this," I say. "Going for a smoke," I add, hot anger still bubbling away inside me, my appetite gone. I get up, grab my jacket and Vincent's cigarettes that are lying next to his smartphone on the table and walk out.

6

"That's his plan," I say.

No point in saying how much I object to it. Zuki got the gist of how I feel about being sent to perform this so-called audit, and, after the birth of our child, being sent to work within Canarus in the capacity as an *advisor* for God knows how long.

"You'll be an advisor, or consultant if you prefer. You won't be on the payroll, don't worry. You'll be there performing advisory tasks to the management – that'll be the official wording. Gunter agreed." Alexis explained this whilst we were sitting at the airport gate waiting to board our flight back to Cyprus. "You're my *banking man*, Neil, just like Michalis was my numbers man. You have experience working in a bank and you'll be better able to assess how they work more than anyone else. You'll be quicker at getting a feel for things and how we might be able to grasp the potential for our secret ventures." Here he winked at me and slapped my shoulder. "You'll be able to spot any discrepancies a lot sooner than anybody else. Just do the audit first, have a good poke around, then we can decide on the loan, and you'll be home in plenty of time for the child's birth."

I admit he took his time to explain his point of view and the necessity of doing an audit, but I was still in a huff about the whole thing and didn't respond much apart from nodding an occasional yes as he extolled my competencies in performing this particular task. But I knew full well, despite my inner turmoil, that in a *family* you perform any role that is asked of you. I knew Alexis was expecting this of me. And Zuki, too, ultimately; although I was certain that she wouldn't be happy about it. And so, I had accepted my fate once more but, in this case, more than reluctantly. The thing that troubles me, apart from having to spend time away from Zuki and the baby, once it's born, is that I have no idea whatsoever about how to assess the functioning of a bank. True, I had worked several years for Hamlays, but only in their asset finance team and purely in a sales and account management role. That hardly qualifies me to conduct an audit of the intricate and multifaceted aspects of a bank.

Canarus has an asset finance division, that much is true, and I might be able to form an opinion about the workings of *that* business. I know my way around loans and lease contracts to finance machines, vehicles and construction equipment. I know that is Canarus's business too, because we checked them out thoroughly before robbing them. But I have no idea about the other types of business Canarus does: private banking, wealth management, cash management, not to speak of such activities like credit and risk management and treasury, accounting and whatever else a bank does behind the scenes. I have no idea about these things, and it will take months if not years to learn. I feel totally overwhelmed by Alexis's expectations.

"I mean, how am I supposed to form an opinion on these aspects? I'm not an accountant or auditor. I don't have the faintest clue. And what if I miss something or they withhold vital information from me and I don't even notice? How do I explain that, especially if Alexis decides to put in twenty million or more?" I can hear the undertone of plaintive wailing in my voice. I know I'm repeating what I've said several times already, but I'm totally at a loss. And I don't even want to think about the moral aspects that still bother me. After all, this is the bank we robbed just six months ago.

"Well," Zuki says, stroking her belly with one hand and squeezing my hand with the other, "for a start I don't think Alexis expects you to perform miracles. He knows you're not a trained auditor. He wants you to look around and get a feeling for how things work and how they're performed. More than anything it's forming an educated opinion, especially of the people. The staff and, more importantly, the Borrells. And, they have a balance sheet, don't they? And a profit and loss statement. Use that as your guideline. Get them to go through each and every line in those statements and insist they explain it all to you in detail. They will hardly refuse."

Okay, I admit that sounds like a sensible approach. I have to concede that much but don't say so. I'm still indulging myself on my righteous indignation given that Alexis wants to send me to Germany whilst Zuki's pregnancy is reaching its critical phase. And, whilst performing an audit is daunting enough, the other aspect really makes my nerves tingle. I feel sick at the prospect of going to work within the bank for an unspecified time and with the very same people we robbed of ten million. To me it feels like performing an autopsy on the person we brutally maimed and murdered. And talking of maiming, I still have the fresh impression of Ralph etched into my mind. I'm wary of him and his odd behaviour, especially towards me. I can't push the gut feeling away that he suspects or knows something. God knows how. It shouldn't be possible given the care with which Gilbert covered our tracks, but the impression was there, and it won't go away. The prospect of being close to someone like that and having to depend on his cooperation to fulfil Alexis's expectations gives me goose bumps.

I take Zuki's hand. "But the worst thing – the absolutely worst thing – my love, is being away from you. And little Matt."

"No way, Neil!" Zuki laughs. "We're not calling him Matt!" she says in mock horror.

"But why not?" I say, laughing also. It's a little running joke we've established thinking up horrible names for our child. "Matt is a great name. I'll settle for Hugh or Ian too."

She blows a raspberry at me. "No, if it's a boy it will be Justin, or Jasper," she says, laughing. "If it's a girl, Jasmine."

"Jasmine? Actually, that *is* a nice name," I say. Jasmine Wilson sounds nice to me.

"Jasmine Epica?" Zuki arches her eyebrows in mock horror.

"Jasmine Epica sounds grand," I say, grinning.

Zuki withdraws her hand and hits me on the arm. "Certainly not Epica," she says, meaning it too.

"Well, we're stuck with that, unless we ask Alexis to buy us a new name. Something grand, like Mountbatten, or Saint John, or…or…" I can't think of any other grand sounding names.

"McManaman," Zuki replies, and we have a good laugh at that.

Zuki gets up, heading for the bathroom, as she constantly does now. She stops at the bathroom door and turns to me. "I know, Neil. I feel awful about it, too. I don't want you to go either," she says, and I can feel the distress she's feeling at the prospect of it. "I don't want us to be like it was for my dad and Naomi."

Naomi, her mother, separated from Michalis because of the demands that working for Alexis brought with it. Naomi moved back to California, leaving Zuki and Sakura to grow up torn between two worlds, and literally worlds apart, drifting back and forth between Cyprus, or wherever Michalis was working, and California.

I sometimes wonder if that's the reason why Zuki chose to be absorbed into Alexis's world, actively becoming a part of it, but by doing so, having a reason to stay here so that we can be together, as a family. I have said to her that there are options. We can leave, maybe live in America like Sakura and Gilbert. Both decided to leave Cyprus and thereby leave Alexis's world – a world that revolves around him and that he absolutely dominates. But Zuki is reluctant to consider this, torn between her desire to keep us together and her desire to be there for Alexis, whom she owes so much. I can see how much it troubles her. There isn't much scope in this family to sit on the fence. You have to decide to be in or to be out.

Whilst Zuki is in the bathroom, I feel the gloom returning. Alexis expects me to fly back out to Düsseldorf as soon as possible and conduct that first audit. Three or four days he said, but I know that won't be enough, and to him the number of days I need to perform my task is irrelevant. He expects a comprehensive first audit, and if it takes two weeks, then so be it. Then I can come back and be here for the birth of our child. But and I've come to realise there's always a *but* working for Alexis, as soon as that's done, he then wants me to go back over to Düsseldorf again to perform that deep dive into the guts of the beast, ostensibly to perform a detailed check and to learn the workings of a bank. His agreement with Gunter is based on this. The first ten million if I'm satisfied after the first audit that his investment is safe and the rest, whatever he is prepared to put in, depending on how satisfied I am with the results of my deep dive. That's the deal he said. But apart from checking that Canarus is healthy as an operational bank, as the basis for his investment, what he really wants is for me to find out how we can use Canarus for our own benefit. That is the clearly stated purpose of his investment: control and influence.

"Just imagine how sweet it will be to use the bank for our purposes," he said to me at the airport whilst we were waiting at the gate. "We will channel our German business through it. The cash flow from our operational business and, once we are set up, the flow of money from our special projects."

But that's not a job to be done in a couple of weeks. That will take many months. Months in which I'll be away from Zuki and little Matt. Zuki doesn't know but in truth, I like the name Matt. Matt Wilson. Kind of cool. With a name like that he can be anything he wants to be.

Düsseldorf airport is quiet on this Sunday afternoon. Perhaps that's why the border police officers checking the passports are taking their time. With not much else to do they critically examine everyone's passport. The line is moving slowly – very slowly. I keep an eye on the automatic passport readers to the side of the booths, but they are out of action and remain so. I wait in line as frustrated as all the other passengers waiting in the long line to move past this obstacle.

"Epica?" the officer says, scrutinising my passport from behind the reinforced glass of his cubicle. "That's an unusual name." He looks at me with an almost challenging stare.

"It is, but it happens," I say, shrugging. He gives me a quizzical look.

"You were born in Cyprus?" he asks, flicking backwards and forwards through my crisp new passport.

"Yes," I answer, not knowing why this should be worth asking – it says so in the passport. I refrain from volunteering any other information. The history of Jordan Epica is complete; Alexis made sure of that. I could tell the border police officer a lot about Jordan Epica. Born thirty years ago to an English ex-serviceman and a Greek Cypriot wife. The schools I went to in Cyprus, the date I got my driving licence and a lot more. But I don't.

The officer reinserts my passport into his machine, but I can't imagine it's showing him anything he hasn't already seen on the screen. Bored now with his perusal of my document and not being able to find any flaws, he hands it back to me and waves me through with a condescending flick of his hand. Arrogant bastard, I think, but I am relieved that my passport is faultless. Grateful for his dismissal, I move through.

It's a hot and humid June afternoon in Düsseldorf and after reclaiming my suitcase I grab a taxi, grateful for its air conditioning. Gunter has arranged a hotel for me close to the Altstadt, perhaps thinking that a young man like me will want to be where the nightlife is. When I get there the hotel turns out to be a dump. Built in the sixties is my guess, and sixties charm it has. A grey structure, with a pebble-coated concrete façade, purely functional with no charm. As I walk into the building with my bag my mood worsens even more. A tasteless reception area, worn and tired looking. The sixties was probably the last time the interior saw a coat of paint too. I doubt they would have dared to put Alexis in a place like this. It just adds to how miserable I currently feel.

I sling my case onto the bed, pull the ghastly orange and brown curtains aside and open the window wide, trying to replace the musty air in the room with some fresher air from outside. But no luck. Below, a four-lane main thoroughfare connects the north and the south of the city and the traffic noise is stupendous, not to mention the smell of exhaust fumes rising up in the humid air. The heat in the room makes me feel like I'm in a sauna. Annoyed, I shut the window, grab my wallet and room key, and commence on an aimless wander through the old town and the city.

On another day, given a different reason for being here, perhaps with Zuki, I'd have enjoyed the walk along the wide promenade by the Rhine, looking out over the big river, swollen from the heavy rains, with its bars and restaurants and the parks dotted around. But not today. Today I feel angry and resentful. Even the altbier tastes bitter, failing to refresh me and my mood. I find an Irish pub, go inside, and am at least mollified by the familiar sound of English, Irish and American voices. The décor of the pub is designed to give the appearance of being authentic Irish, whatever that is, but fails in achieving this. It has the charm of a franchise system, but I don't care.

I take a stool at the bar, grateful for the air conditioning and order a Kilkenny. I sip the beer, idly watching a Premier League football game, even if it's a repeat that's running on the numerous flat screens hanging in each corner of the pub. Two blokes enter and take the stools beside me. They're speaking English. As they glance at me, I nod a hello.

"All right, mate," one of them says to me in a broad London accent, and it brings a smile to my face. I feel back at home in England.

"Yeah, sure," I answer. "Good to hear English voices."

"You look like you need another, mate," the man says.

"Yeah, and another after that. What you having?" I say, happy for some company and conversation.

They look me up and down, exchange a glance, and I can see I pass muster as they settle at the bar, willing to engage in conversation with me.

"Same as you," the first man says. I turn to other man, and he nods a yes.

"Two pints of Kilkenny, then," I say and place the order with the barman.

In the time the barman pulls the pints, I turn to my new drinking companions. "I'm Neil. Nice to meet you," I say.

"Chris," the first man says, "and that's Cliff."

Chris is the older of the two. Mid-forties I'd guess, with short brown hair, streaked through with grey. Medium height and square framed. A genuine Cockney, he says proudly, and he looks like ex-army or a rugby player, maybe. Cliff has ginger hair, with a freckled face. He's tall and slim, and, so he says, from Essex. The barman places the beers on the bar. "Cheers," I say.

"Cheers," they echo, and we take a thirsty gulp.

"So, what brings you here, Neil?" Chris asks.

"Business," I reply. "And you?"

"Oh, we're both telecom engineers with Vodafone."

"Vodafone?"

"Yeah, they have their regional head office here in Düsseldorf. Massive place, on the other side of the Rhine."

We drink and talk, the conversation flowing easily. I feel my spirits rise as the beers do their bit and the banter moves back and forth. We order food, burger and greasy chips – the staple diet of the Anglo-American nations.

"What lies between fear and sex?" Cliff asks after what seems like a couple of hours.

"Dunno," both Chris and I reply.

"*Fünf*," he says with a drunken grin. *(Five.)* "Five pints is enough for me. I'm outta here," he announces.

I look at my watch – it's coming up to 11 p.m. Jeez, we've been drinking and chatting since 7 p.m. "Better call it a day – early start tomorrow," I say, my tongue slightly tangled and my speech just a little bit slurred. "Been a great evening. Thanks, lads."

I step outside and into air even more sticky than before. Waiting for Chris and Cliff, I pull out my phone to check for any messages I might have missed. Nothing, which is good. A movement on the other side of the cobbled lane registers in my brain, and I look up to see two men emerge from the shadows of a doorway opposite. Slim figures, dressed uniformly in jeans, trainers and hoodies. They look like trouble, so my brain throws a switch. I'm instantly alert.

Their movement is purposeful – this spells trouble. I put my phone in my back pocket and go into what Vincent calls street fighting mode. I stand easy but my muscles tense up, ready for confrontation. The taller of the two comes straight towards me. The smaller guy veers left, circling to get behind me. The guy heading for me, face buried deep under his hood, picks up his stride, and I just know he's coming in to head-butt me.

I move my upper body back and lower my head, keeping my eyes on him, gauging the timing of his movements. Vincent taught me a lesson or two on how to fight. He's an expert in close quarter fighting skills and a martial arts form called *capoeira carioca*. It's something he learnt in his younger years and apart from some funny dance-like moves, it's a no-nonsense variety. No thrills – just hard and dirty. He's shown me how to parry a head-butt, and now I'm grateful to him.

The man doesn't break stride as he walks into me, head moving forcefully forward. I lean further back, lowering my head, protecting my nose. He overextends, the blow not connecting, and I slam my knee up into his groin. He groans with the impact. I thrust my hands forward, thumbs out and dig them into his eyes. He screams, and I shove him backwards as hard as I can. He slams onto the ground, writhing, with one hand to his groin and the other to his eyes.

During this I hear a commotion behind me and the smashing of glass – a bottle being hit against a wall? My brain hasn't forgotten the threat of the smaller man, now somewhere behind me, outside of my vision. I begin to turn, Vincent's instructions from our training sessions forcing themselves into my head: *stand side-on, reduce the area you expose to your assailant.*

Before I've completed the turn, I hear a voice – Chris's. "Oi… No you don't, you little fuck!" he says, followed by the sound of a fist smacking into bone. As I turn around, I see Chris's extended arm, fist clenched, and the smaller man crashing onto the ground, blood gushing from his nose, a broken bottle neck rolling into the gutter.

We stand, prepared for more, but the assailants have had enough. The taller man gets to his knees and stands up, bending double in pain. He stumbles in a blind zigzag across to the other man, helps him up and supporting each other, they flounder away into the shadows of the night.

"What was that all about?" Chris asks, dragging his eyes away from their retreating backs to look at me with a puzzled expression.

"God knows," I answer equally puzzled by the events. "I was checking my phone. Can't believe they were after my phone. It's an ancient model," I say, holding it up for both to see.

"He was going to go for you with that bottle," he says. "Bit drastic just for a phone."

"Perhaps they wanted to mug you?" Cliff says. "They went straight for you," he adds after a moment.

"Mug me? But I have nothing worth robbing." I find that hard to believe, especially right in front of a pub in the middle of the old town, but then again, perhaps that was their crazy intent.

"Where's your hotel?" Chris asks.

"Not far. Round there somewhere," I answer, pointing vaguely in the direction I remember the hotel to be.

"We'll walk you back and take a taxi from there. They could be waiting for you round the corner," Chris says.

***

"Why didn't you ring?" Zuki says when I call her the next morning.

"Didn't want to wake you, my love," I reply. The truth is I didn't want to upset her given the events of last night, so I restricted my report to the unbearable heat in the room. I couldn't sleep, the room stiflingly hot without air conditioning and my brain ceaselessly replaying the pointless attack. I'd taken a shower and lain down on the bed with the window open, warm air enveloping me and trying to shut out the noise from the traffic below. Within minutes, I was soaking wet from the sweat pouring out, no closer to understanding the motive behind the attack, and grateful for Chris's strong right arm, stopping the smaller man from causing severe injuries with that broken bottle. What the hell? Baffled and shocked, I must have drifted off to sleep at some point, waking with a sore head and unsteady nerves.

"Oh dear. I'm sure things will get better. And if all else fails, find another hotel," Zuki says.

"Yes, I'll do that," I say, conceding to myself that sensible and easy solution. After getting up, I'd showered again, finishing off by standing a full minute under ice-cold water, pushing the nasty experience aside. Nothing to be done apart from focussing on the task that Alexis has given me, even if I still feel it's a god-awful thing he's thrust upon me. The shower freshened me up, and I now I get myself ready. I put on my freshly laundered and pressed suit, polished black shoes, and select a tie, which I stuff into my inside pocket.

With my foul mood and frayed nerves washed away, I feel an odd sense of excitement and dread rolled into one now that I'm here and will soon be entering Canarus bank. I check the directions on my smartphone once more and set off on foot, laptop bag over my shoulder.

Canarus bank's premises are a ten-minute walk from the hotel, and at least the morning air is fresher. The arrangement is for me to present myself at nine in the morning and as I'm early I take a tour around the building, discovering a little Italian café on the opposite side of the road. It's open, serving coffee and pastries to the early morning commuters and coffee-to-go clientele. Armed with a cappuccino and a couple of croissants, I sit down in a corner with a good view of Canarus's main entrance.

Canarus bank is located close to the stock exchange and in one of the few old buildings left standing in the financial district. I remember reading the building survived the bombing of World War Two, one of the few buildings in the commercial centre to do so. Flanked on each side by soulless glass and concrete office complexes, the Canarus bank building stands out like a sore thumb, but in a positive way. Its reddish-brown sandstone façade, with its columns and artful details, is an echo of long-gone times. I can only guess, but I'd say it was built before the First World War, a time they call the Wilhelmian era, sometime between 1890 and 1918.

I watch as staff members come, entering the bank by a side door next to the main doors, which are accessed by climbing several steps, no doubt at the time designed to instil humbleness and fear into the customers that deigned to enter the mighty banking hall. Whilst I sit and watch the Canarus bank employees enter by the former tradesman's entrance, I wonder if Kerstin is still an employee, and whether she might have just entered the bank before my very eyes. But I doubt it, she would have been sacked for her breach of conduct that after all enabled us to pull off the digital hit-and-run last November. There would have been no room for leniency given the severity of her breach and the damage caused.

"Time to face the enemy," I say to myself after checking my watch for the hundredth time. I get up, pay for my coffee and croissants, and walk across the road to the main entrance. It's exactly 9 a.m. as I stride up the steps and into the main banking hall.

The hall is a sight to behold. Marble floors, marble-clad columns and a high dome with its glass skylight – a sign of the wealth that banks accrued in the grand old days, and which they invested in themselves. I stand just inside the entrance taking it all in before noticing a man walking towards me, a big smile in place and his arm already extending forward to greet me.

"Punctual to the minute," Oliver Borrell says as he shakes my hand.

"Of course," I reply, a smile fixing itself into position.

"Did you have a good trip and a good first night?" he asks, and I just nod in affirmation. "Take in the Altstadt last night?" he asks.

"Just for something to eat and a few beers," I reply, keeping the misery I felt to myself.

We have passed through the banking hall by this point, and we're stopped by a secured glass door. Oliver swipes his key card on a reader and pulls the heavy door open. He waves me through, and we walk down a corridor, our shoes loud on the polished tiled floor. He guides me to a lift, pleasantries now exchanged and both of us left with nothing else to say for the time being.

The lift takes us up to the sixth floor. We walk out into an open-plan space with a reception area. It registers with me that this is where the Canarus's gods reside, not unlike the top floor of Hamlays in London where my short career as key account manager once began. All ancient history now. He leads me into his office, which is dominated by a vast, highly polished black desk with several phones and monitors arrayed on it. He guides me to a round glass and chrome table in a corner. Four leather chairs, chrome coffee flask and a little plate of biscuits are set out on the glass top. We sit, he offers me coffee, busies himself with pouring, offering sugar and milk, and then leans back looking at me, expectation on his face. I hold his look, thank him for the coffee and take a long time taking a sip.

I surreptitiously take in his office. He has some nice paintings on the walls, black-framed colourful modern works, and they look like originals too. On the sideboard behind his desk, I spot some classy black and white photos, most probably taken by a professional photographer, of what looks like his wife and two young kids from this distance.

"What's your role in Canarus?" I ask him.

He hesitates for a second, and I can sense him contemplating his answer. Not the only one to have undergone some extended briefings, I think to myself, remembering the peptalk Alexis subjected me to before I set off to the airport. He decides on his answer and says, "I'm the managing director of Canarus's asset finance division. Primarily for the front-end activities – you know, sales and marketing."

"Really," I say, interested now seeing this is the territory I'm familiar with and, coincidentally, it's the business we targeted for our cyber-attack. "That's interesting."

"Is it?" he says, and I can see some surprise on his face.

"Yes, I worked in asset finance myself," I say before I can stop myself. Damn, I think, and he's *very* interested now.

"In which capacity and where?"

I should have kept my mouth shut, but it was an impulse that made me say it. I can't divulge any details – certainly not that I worked at Hamlays. He'll know all about Hamlays and the fraud that occurred there not even two years ago. That will certainly set his alarm bells off, especially as I remember that Canarus was also affected by the Holden Industrial scandal, being one of the major funders of their equipment in Germany.

"Oh, I started my career working for a broker many years ago," I lie. "And what is Ralph's role here in the bank?" I ask, keen to change the topic.

"Ralph is the managing director of the private banking and wealth management business. You know, the affluent private customers with more money than sense," he says, and again I can perceive that wariness deep down that he has of his brother. He sees something in my expression. "You know he does all the stockbroking stuff. Like me, from a front-end perspective, sales and marketing. He's very good with our established private clientele," he says, and I nod my head, myself now feeling a similar wariness that I'll have to face him when I get round to looking into that side of the bank's activities.

"So, how's the bank's management setup?" I ask.

"Well, there's my father, Gunter Borrell, whom you met. He's the majority shareholder and chairman of the board, or CEO if you prefer. Then we have Doctor Burkhard Linnemann, he's the managing director or board executive responsible for the back-end functions of the bank. That includes risk management, risk controlling, treasury, and so forth.

"And then there's Martin Lambeck, the third managing director or board member, responsible for IT and all organisational aspects. These three form the management board. Then we have Ralph and me, both managing directors for our respective business lines. And then the other department heads that together make up the management committee. I have prepared some documents for you," he says, reaching behind and picking up a folder that is lying on his desk. He hands it over, and I glance at the first pages. Lying on the top is an organisational chart and behind that, pages with detailed information and financial performance data from the various business areas. Okay, so they do have a presentation, I think to myself. I put it to one side and smile at him.

"Where do you want to start?" he asks me.

Bloody good question, I think. Where the hell does one start? I have no clue of what I should be doing and in which order, but I can't let him see that.

"Oh, we usually start with the back-end operations," I say, making it sound grand and as if I know what the hell I'm doing. I'm just glad he can't see beyond the façade. "But perhaps we can meet the board members first?"

"Of course," he says. "We'll start with Doctor Linnemann and then Herr Lambeck. My father is away on business, and so is Ralph, so you won't meet them until Wednesday," he adds, and I can't say I'm saddened by that fact, especially where Ralph is concerned.

"*Doctor* Linnemann?" I ask, wondering if Canarus has a medical man on the board.

"Yes, Doctor Linnemann. He has a Ph.D., and – well, you might not be aware of it – the title of 'doctor' is used quite a bit over here as a prefix to the name." He sees my quizzical look. "Well, most academics tend to use it. It makes them feel elevated and helps getting a table in busy restaurants, apparently. The doctor is an academic title of which he is very proud," he says, a small timid humorous smile spreading across his lips. I smile back at him.

"Oh, and do I need to bear anything in mind concerning this…er…audit?" I ask, remembering just in time that my task might well be confidential as far as the Borrells are concerned.

"Yes, good that you mention it," he says, apparently having forgotten that aspect, too. "My father has informed the board members and department heads that you are here as an advisor from a consultancy firm to perform an audit of our systems and processes following the events of last

November. To give us a clean bill of health, so to speak." He smiles. "It sounds authentic enough, but you should refrain from providing any further information. If anybody asks just refer them to us."

Having sorted that out, we make our way to Doctor Linnemann's office. Oliver knocks on the office door and opens it a fraction, peeping round to address the man. Such subservience seems a main trait of his character. I guess that Ralph would just boldly march in.

He beckons me to enter and, pushing the door open to let me in, I see a tall, thin man with a gaunt face, receding hair and wearing a worn, crumpled grey suit standing at his raised computer. He turns towards me, pushing his spectacles up onto his forehead. Now that I can see him full on, I wonder how old he is. He could be forty, he could be sixty – it's difficult to say. He could be an old-looking young man or vice versa.

"Guten Tag, Herr…" He pauses for just a moment. "Epica?"

"Jordan Epica," I say, walking up to him to shake his hand. His grip is so limp, his hand like warm jelly, that I fight the urge to wipe my hand on my trousers.

"Ja," he says, switching to English. "So, so, you are here to gain an informed impression of our bank."

"Exactly," I say.

"And what can I tell you, Herr Epica?"

"Well, I think this is primarily an introduction, but I would certainly like to gain an impression of the departments that report to you. And, of course, I'd appreciate if you would, if necessary, add any information that might become necessary during the course of my audit." Sounds professional enough to my ears, so I hope that clinches it, for the time being. But Doctor Linnemann appears grateful for the opportunity to have an audience and launches into a monologue that lasts two hours.

Halfway through he switches to German, totally forgetting that I'm not a fluent German speaker and oblivious to the fact that I'm having difficulties following him. I don't have a clue what he's talking about, but I don't interject, and Oliver, taking his cue from me, resists too. We let him drone on. I use the time to take in his office without making it too obvious, and what I see cements my impression of the man.

His office is a mess, papers strewn everywhere, mostly it appears to be topics unrelated to his role in the bank. I spot a large illustrated book on birds lying open on one side of his desk. Perhaps he's an ornithologist, I think, and examine the office for more signs. He has some pictures of songbirds hanging on the wall, so he could be. I suppress a yawn, the sleepless night catching up with me, wondering how a man in his position can have so much time on his hands. Given that he's the board member responsible for the back-end operations, I'd have expected him to be a stickler for tidiness and regulations, just like his counterpart at Hamlays, but apparently not. Finally finished, he brings the meeting to an abrupt end and dismisses us.

Next, I'm introduced to Martin Lambeck, the board member responsible for IT and all organisational aspects. This man is what I would have expected Dr Linnemann to be: medium height, early fifties, physically fit with short salt-and-pepper hair and full of energy. Whilst not unfriendly, he's gruffer and more direct. He knows my name and the purpose of my visit.

"If that's okay for you, I will call you Jordan. Your surname is quite unusual," he says in very good English with a slight American twang. He looks me directly in the eyes with an expression of curiosity as he asks the question I'm slowly getting used to. And why am I not surprised? "Is that a common name in Cyprus?"

"No, it's not a common name anywhere in the world," I answer, thinking I will have to talk to Alexis. We need to change it; it's attracting too much attention.

"Okay," he says, the issue of my name now closed. "As you will be aware, we were targeted by cyber criminals last November." I nod my head in confirmation, having expected Dr Linnemann to have raised this topic. "The criminals were able to breach our IT security and exploited a bug in the software we didn't know existed. We have updated the system and are suing the software company for not having advised us about the risk of this flaw in the system. Our IT is Fort Knox now – that much I can assure you."

I make a show of nodding eagerly, showing him that on behalf of my employers and my task here I very much approve of this information.

"Furthermore, we have tightened all aspects of internal compliance and adherence to our policies. The person that, albeit unwittingly, enabled these gangsters to rob us was sacked and all employees have been informed in clear terms that any breach will lead to immediate dismissal, loss of all pension benefits and prosecution for damages."

I feel a pang of remorse, shame and guilt, and my heart goes out to poor Kerstin. I can only guess what she's doing now; I hope she's surviving.

"Anything else?" he asks, making it clear that *his* time is valuable.

"No, I think that covers what I needed to know," I say. "If I may consult with you on any issues or questions that arise, I'd be grateful," I add, thinking that this is in line, too, with what I as an auditor should ask.

"If you must, but I think my staff will be able to answer any questions you might have most competently," he says, dismissing me. And that's it.

As we take our leave, I wonder what Mr Lambeck thinks of Doctor Linnemann. Out of curiosity I ask Oliver out in the corridor, "Dr Linnemann, what's his Ph.D. in?"

"I think it was something to do with ornithology," he answers, and again I can't help but feel that Dr Linnemann is where he is because of his incompetence.

"How long has he been here? At Canarus?"

"Let me think," Oliver replies. "Twenty-plus years, I guess."

I suppress my urge to ask him how he managed to keep hold of his job given that the breach was within the departments he's responsible for.

"And Mr Lambeck?"

"Mr Lambeck has been with the bank ten years or more, but was appointed to the position last year, following the…er…events and dismissal of the IT chief," he says.

And I'm not surprised at that. Strictly speaking I suppose one can argue that the cyber-attack was successful because of a flaw in the IT system, coupled with a breach of policy, and hence not exactly in Dr Linnemann's area of responsibility. He was probably lucky to survive in his position, but it adds weight to what I thought earlier on. Often enough, and here I'm recalling what Alexis said about the Borrells being rogues, it pays to have a, how should I call it, more *pliable* member on the board. I make a mental note to keep my eyes open for any signs that support my theory. As for Martin Lambeck, I can't think of him being pliable, but you never know. Everyone has his price – as I well know.

I spend the rest of the day talking to the department heads of the back-end functions: risk controlling, compliance, finance and accounting, and treasury. Whilst I learn a lot about how the bank works and how much red tape and regulation exist, especially since the events of last November, there is nothing that seems unusual or worthy of any further investigation. The department heads of these departments are just like those at Hamlays: boring.

One notable exception is the head of the credit department, a guy called Peter Aulmann. A man in his mid-forties and with an attitude. He fixes me with hostile eyes as soon as I walk into his office. His stance is thrusting, and I get the impression he's eager to come across as lean and mean – or maybe he *is* just mean. In any case, he's a guy who smiles a lot but doesn't mean it. He makes it obvious, right from the start, that he's very distrustful of me and wary to provide any detailed insight. Perhaps it's just his nature, but I can't help but wonder if his briefing has been more thorough than that of the other department heads. Or he's just obnoxious by nature. He ponders and challenges each of my questions before answering. More often than not, he *asks* me questions, especially of the sort, *"Why do you want to know?"*

Especially as we touch on the credit scoring tools that Canarus use in their small- and mid-ticket business. IT-based scoring tools to assess the creditworthiness and to automate the credit decisions of small transactions are common throughout the banking industry, and it's only mild curiosity on my part, resulting from my experience at Hamlays, that lets me bring up the topic altogether. But Peter Aulmann has no interest in expanding on the subject.

"Why is this of relevance to you?" he asks.

"It's not particularly relevant," I concede. "Mere curiosity on my part," I admit. "I've had some dealings with such systems in the past and just wondered how it's put to use here."

He takes a long time deliberating an answer, staring at me all the time whilst he thinks his answer through, smile fixed but eyes boring into me. He's probably weighing up if he can tell me to go fuck myself but, in the end, and probably making allowance for my role, he says, preceded by a long sigh, "Well, if you want to see how it works, I guess there's no harm in showing you." He arranges for me to spend some time in the credit department, so that's where I spend the remaining two hours of day one.

I'm escorted to the credit team by a young lady whom he summons and explains briefly what to show me. Her name is Jasmin, which I find touching.

The way he pronounces it, though, with the emphasis on the first syllable, makes it sound hard. But again, perhaps it's just me, and the fact that I have decided not to like Mr Aulmann. By now he, too, has earnt himself an entry in my notebook worthy of further scrutiny.

Jasmin is a young and attractive woman in her twenties. She's of medium height, a bit taller than Zuki. Long blonde hair and slim. She smiles a lot, in a demure way, and takes me to her desk in an open-plan area, the usual potted plants and screens providing some soundproofing and privacy. I nod my hello to several other employees sitting at their desks eyeing me curiously as we walk by.

We sit down at her desk, which she keeps neat and tidy, and she shows me her job. She's a junior credit underwriter, she tells me, and her task is to process incoming credit applications from Canarus's numerous partners in the retail business. She explains that Canarus has many retail partners that they cooperate with, primarily in the hi-tech sector, which for them is medical apparatus, telecommunication, IT and office equipment. She goes on to explain that these partners sell their equipment to their corporate customer base and provide a financing offer too. If the customers are interested in the offered financing, then the retailer submits the financing request via a web-based tool. It's straightforward stuff, similar to what we did at Hamlays.

"The financing requests are relayed via a web tool by the retailers and pop up in the credit system," Jasmin explains, clicking on her computer mouse, scrolling through various screens. "The tool triggers the credit approval process automatically and the scoring system generates a recommendation, based on the databases we use, which I then validate. I can approve based on the tool's recommendation, or I can decline, or I can refer for further evaluation. That's when I take a close look at the file."

It's familiar to me, but I let Jasmin explain. I'm intrigued to find out that Canarus's scoring tool can, in theory, approve a transaction up to an amount of five hundred thousand euros. That is a lot more than Hamlays' system was configured to do.

"Well," Jasmin explains, "the scoring system is based on a complex system of interlinked databases, and the algorithms have been perfected over time. So, the system is able to handle transactions of that magnitude. But we don't have many financing requests of that size, though. The majority are in the range of twenty to fifty thousand euros." She reels it off automatically, a speech she has learnt well over time, smiling at me as the words flow from her mouth, and I realise she has no clue whatsoever of what the machine is doing in the background.

I ask her what the overall approval rate is, and she states, with some pride in her voice, "It's over eighty per cent." Impressive, and certainly a higher approval rate than Hamlays, at least as far as I remember. She shows me some more referrals that pop up on her screen and after ten more files, I get the picture.

On her desk are some printed-out credit files and I pick up one, flicking through it. It's a referral from the morning, which, so she explains, she approved and has printed off before passing it on for processing. She tells me that despite the approval process being automated, the credit decision and credit report from the database plus the rating score are printed out and put into a file. So much for saving paper, I can't help but think.

"The file is then passed on to the processing department until the loan or lease is finalised, paid out and then the complete documentation is stored digitally," she tells me in her prim and proper way. Mr Aulmann must be proud of you, I think.

I'm just being nosy, nothing more, and I glance through the credit application. It's a transaction referred by an IT retailer for a business loan to finance IT equipment for a medium-sized company. Standard stuff; nothing out of the ordinary. One hundred and fifty thousand euros to be funded over forty-eight months. A big deal, then. Wondering what a hundred and fifty grand would buy in IT equipment, I flick through the pages looking for the specifics. Some pages later I find the specs: software and servers plus desktops and laptops. Okay, I think, sounds boring but plausible.

I flick through the pages, but there's nothing more to see. I notice the retailer has a credit rating too and there's a star next to the name.

"What's the star for?"

"Oh, that means that the retailer—" she leans over to read the name "—CompuTel IT, is a star partner."

"A star partner?"

"Yes, we have different categories for the retailers that work with us. The more business they refer, the higher their ranking and partner status. Star partner is the best category. Minimum one million euro per annum of referred business," she says. "They get special treatment," she adds with another smile in place. I'm sure they do, I think to myself.

Oliver walks in. "Ah, Jordan, come to relieve you. I hope you've had a good day."

"Great, thanks." I consult my watch to see it's coming up to 5 p.m.

"Thought we might get together for dinner," he says.

"If you have time," I say, remembering the photos on his sideboard. "That's if your wife doesn't mind, and the kids."

"Oh, Julia won't mind," he replies. "In fact, I said to her this morning I'd probably be taking you out this evening."

"Great."

"I'll pick you up at seven? Outside your hotel?"

8

Come 7 p.m. Oliver is waiting for me outside the hotel's glass-fronted entrance. I've had just enough time to ring Zuki and have a quick shower. Not being able to get hold of Alexis, I text him to let him know that the first day went okay. *All well, nothing out of the ordinary to report*, I'd written.

It's another unusually hot and humid evening, and we decide to take a slow stroll into the Altstadt. "Monday evening is usually quieter," he says, but there's loads of people outside the pubs and restaurants. I decline his suggestion to go into one of the big traditional breweries as it's hot enough outside and, despite the vast cavernous hall, the heat inside is unbearable. We find a Spanish restaurant in a lane off the pedestrian zone and sit down at a table outside, ordering various tapas.

"How did your first day go?" he asks me after our beers are placed before us and we both take large sips, wiping the froth from our lips.

"That's good," I say, enjoying the cold Pils beer.

He smiles at me. "Better than your beer in Cyprus?"

"Oh, beer in Cyprus is no worse. We have Pils and we have all the other beers the world has on offer too," I reply.

"You were born in Cyprus?" he asks, but I'm instantly back on guard.

"Yes," I say.

"Your English sounds British English rather than…" But he fails to find the words he's looking for. "Cypriot English" is I guess what he had in mind.

"I was born in Cyprus, but I'm of English descent," I tell him. "I went to boarding school in England, so I'm as native and fluent as everybody else," I lie. Risky territory too as Jordan Epica's background does not have any time spent at an English boarding school. I'm glad the first tapas dishes arrive, hoping we can turn the conversation to other topics. "Your wife's name is Julia?" I ask between bites, eager to change the subject.

"*Ja*," he says, chewing.

"And your kids?"

"Nils and Beatrix," he says. "Seven and five," he adds. "You have children?" he asks, and it momentarily stops me in my tracks.

It's a question I didn't expect to be asked myself. And before I can check myself, it slips out, "Not yet, but in the making."

"Your first?"

"Yes." I can't help but grin.

"How wonderful," he replies, with a knowing smile. "It's a delight," he says. "Most of the time," he adds, and winks at me.

I steer the conversation away from my life. The less he knows the better.

"I guess with two kids, it's a busy life," I say, and he laughs.

"Never a dull moment, as you'll find out."

I keep the conversation going on like this, trivial but informative stuff, nonetheless. Oliver's a pleasant guy, a family man. He seems genuine and has none of the traits his brother displays. I wonder how I can get him to tell me more about Ralph.

"Your brother said you are somehow related to Baron von Richthofen, is that so?"

He looks at me bewildered. "No, that's not so. What made him say that?"

"When we met at your father's house. He said something along those lines. Unless I misheard him," I offer.

"Oh, he probably means Jochen Deselaers."

"Yes, come to think of it, that's the name he mentioned."

"Right. Jochen Deselaers was indeed a pilot in World War One. He's, now let me think, my great-grandfather on my mother's side of the family. The Deselaers originally came from Belgium but moved with the bank to Düsseldorf and over time became German. They are part of the original family that founded Canarus. My mother married into the Borrell family but always kept her maiden name. A, what do you say in English, double surname: Borrell-Deselaers. We still have that in our family name, but we don't use it except for Ralph. But he is more like the Deselaers anyway."

Now I understand the initials on Ralph's elaborate signet ring, RBD: Ralph Borrell-Deselaers.

"Your brother is quite a character," I say trying to keep it light – a general observation, no more.

Oliver gives me a long look, I guess weighing up the comment, but I deliberately ignore his look, helping myself to some more of the tapas. "Yes, that he is," he says after a while but in a guarded way, and I can feel his eyes scrutinising me. For a moment I feel he's going to leave it at that, but after a moment he adds, "We are totally different. Opposites if that's the correct term."

We eat some more food in silence, and I don't push him. Let him add more if he wants to.

"He's the spitting image of my mother," he says after a while. "Impulsive and rash. A narcissist. Charming and considerate one moment and totally imperious and without scruples the next."

Wow, now that's quite a statement, I think to myself. "But good with the wealthy clientele," I say, and he smiles as he recognises his own words.

"*Ja*, very good with the wealthy clientele," he says, nodding. I struggle to find other things I can ask to get more insight, but I can't think of anything else that won't raise his suspicions.

"He has a penthouse just round the corner. A fantastic place. The top three floors with a great view across the Altstadt, the Rhine and the other side of town. It's a funny arrangement," he adds. "It's sort of upside down." Obviously, my look conveys some confusion, for he expands. "You enter the penthouse at the top level and then you go down. You know, the entrance is right at the top, where he has a large roof terrace. In the middle there's an open gallery that goes all the way down, three floors. On the floor below he has several rooms, bedrooms and his own gym. And right at the bottom is the lounge and the kitchen and another terrace with an amazing view over the whole town, the river itself and the other side of the river with the district of Oberkassel."

"Sounds amazing. I'd love to have a look."

"Oh, then we must ask him," he replies, and I think it's the last thing I want to do. "His friend or, how do you say, he's not married?"

"Partner," I volunteer.

"His partner, Elisabeth. She is a great cook and host."

"Elisabeth?" I can't stop myself in time from blurting that out.

He looks up at me, surprise on his face. "Yes, Elisabeth."

"Oh, sorry," I say, wondering what on earth I can say to cover up my blunder. I misunderstood him. "It's just that you said his *friend*. But of course, you meant girlfriend."

Oliver chuckles before replying, "Ralph is so over-the-top masculine that he sometimes comes across as being…" Now it's his turn to trail off not knowing how to put into words what he's thinking without making it sound worse. "He'd kill me for this," he says, laughing, and I join in, another little bond established between us.

After dinner we stroll through the Altstadt and down to the promenade by the Rhine. It's still humid but down by the river it's pleasant enough. The promenade, so Oliver informs me, stretches two kilometres along the eastern bank of the river, from the city's new port development and past the regional parliament all the way to the Rheinterrassen, a large function hall dating from 1924, sporting a large beer garden and an open-air cinema in the summer.

"You can walk even further if you want to," he says, "all the way to the exhibition halls by the airport."

"I'll have to jog along there tomorrow morning, then," I say, and he gives me a look as if he believes me.

Oliver points out several landmarks, the telecommunications tower, 234 metres high with its revolving restaurant and special feature, a digital clock made up of various sets of lights to show the time.

As we stroll along, we pass a tall building. "This is where Ralph has his penthouse," he says, pointing. "The top three floors are his," he says, and we stop to take a look. It's a striking building, a twelve-storey semi-circular structure standing on the corner of the ancient city harbour and the promenade. I can appreciate the view must be fantastic, the top three floors having a massive glass frontage that provides a clear 270-degree view across the Altstadt and the Rhine.

"Not bad," I say in real and honest appreciation.

"Yes, a fantastic property. But not for me. I prefer to live in the hills where the air is fresh and where the deer come into my garden, and the foxes and the hares say goodnight. That's an old German saying," he explains seeing my quizzical look.

We continue our stroll, but I can see he wants to get going, the furtive glances at his watch giving him away. His family is waiting for him.

"Oliver, go home," I say. "It's late. Your family is surely up and waiting for you."

He shakes my hand. "Thank you, Jordan. It's been a very pleasant evening."

For once, and thanks to his genuine and kind manner, "Jordan" doesn't grate in my ears and we say goodbye. A pleasant bloke I concede as I watch him hurry off, and in a different place and setting I'd think he'd be a nice person to spend time with.

I take my time and a circular route back to the hotel. Meandering along the promenade, I stand and watch the fully laden cargo ships, some with barges strapped to their bows, laboriously making their way up river whilst their colleagues, goods delivered, race past in the opposite direction at breakneck speed.

The balmy air is enjoyable now that the humidity has eased and there's an almost Mediterranean feel to the promenade. People are sitting outside, enjoying long drinks or sipping beer, watching the world meander by and the sun slowly starting its descent. I stop for one final altbier, standing at a trestle table outside one of the breweries idly observing the people enjoying their evening out.

With a sigh, I brace myself to face the inevitable: the hot stuffy room, the walk back to the hotel, through the baking lobby and up the stairs to my floor.

Once back, I pause for a moment as I unlock and open the door. The heat and stuffiness of the room envelopes me. I had enjoyed the evening out, the air warm but not too uncomfortable, and now I have to face another sleepless night in this sauna of a room.

As I switch on the lights, I notice an envelope lying on the floor, popped though the gap under my door. I pick it up, my name handwritten on the front. I open the envelope and unfold the piece of paper. I read the typed words: *Start with Weinreich. That's the beginning.*

9

Come 3 a.m. I give up, unable to sleep. I've been tossing and turning in bed, sweating and my mind pondering over the note. I get up and switch on the desk lamp. The envelope and note lie side by side where I left them as I climbed into bed, unable to make any sense of the message. Now, I take the notepad lying on the desk and the cheap biro, sporting the hotel's name, and force my brain into gear, ready to jot my thoughts down:

- *Envelope: name handwritten, first name and surname*
- *Woman's handwriting?*
- *Who sent it?*
- *What does it mean?*

I sit staring at the note. Why should anyone slip a note beneath the door? It must be connected to Canarus. What else should be its purpose? For a start, who knows I'm here? The Borrells obviously. The people I met yesterday within Canarus. But do they know where I'm staying? I suppose they could know or find out easily enough. But why would someone on Canarus's payroll send me a note?

Finding no answer to that riddle, I ponder the first part of the message. *Start with Weinreich.*

Who or what is *Weinreich*? A name, or so it would appear. A person? Perhaps an employee.

Start with Weinreich: Name? Employee? I jot down on the paper.

And what does "Start with Weinreich" mean? I underline the first word. Start with what? As in talk to him? Or her, even. But about what? Doesn't make any sense to me. I look at the second part of the message: *That's the beginning.*

The beginning of what? My mind is in overdrive, trying desperately to make sense of the message but I can't find any clues.

That's the beginning. Beginning of what? I write down.

I get back into bed, frustrated and mentally exhausted from my fruitless pondering. I wonder for a brief moment if there's any connection between the note and the events outside the Irish pub. But it seems absurd. How would an attempted mugging and a note like this be connected? Sleep evades me still, so I lie in bed waiting for the alarm.

***

Standing half hidden behind a column outside the staff entrance I wait and hope. Hoping to spot Jasmin, the young woman from the credit department when

120

she comes to work. I'm in luck and at 7:30 I see her walking up the steps from the underground station. She's wearing a summer dress and her blonde hair, drawn back in a ponytail, sways to the rhythm of her energetic steps. In contrast to me she looks fresh and rested. I time it just right, moving into her path as she walks the last steps towards my position.

"Good morning, Jasmin," I say as she sees me.

"Guten Morgen, Herr Epica," she replies. Her manner is friendly and genuinely unconcerned, so I strike her off my mental list of potential people who might have sent me the message.

"Please, call me Jordan," I say as we move towards the staff entrance.

Jasmin takes out her keycard, holds it against the reader, and I open the door for her.

"Jasmin, I'm too early, couldn't sleep. Do you mind if I join you until Oliver arrives?"

I have no idea when Oliver usually gets into work, but it's Jasmin I want some time with. Time to ask some questions. Jasmin just smiles and nods, and we climb the stairs up to the floor and the as yet deserted open office space where she has her desk. I note with some satisfaction, as we pass the offices along the corridor, that her boss, Peter Aulmann, hasn't arrived yet either.

Jasmin starts up her computer and monitors, gets herself and me a coffee from the small kitchen and we sit down at her desk.

"Jasmin," I ask, trying to make the question I have lined up sound innocent. "Do you have anybody working here called Weinreich?"

"No," she replies. "Never heard of that name amongst the staff. But I'll check."

She turns to her computer and enters the name. "No, no one with the name Weinreich in the system."

I scrutinise her reaction and facial expression as best as I can without it becoming obvious, just in case she is covering up something, but she shows no reaction.

"How is the name written?" I ask.

She shoots me a quizzical look, but is kind enough to grab a piece of paper and writes the name down. Looking at her handwriting, I'm convinced now that she can't have written the name on the envelope. Fortunately, she doesn't ask me why I want to know all this. We sit drinking our coffee, and I try to engage her in some casual conversation. How long have you been working at Canarus? Where do you live? That kind of stuff. I can see that she wants to get started on her work and I'm just wasting her time. I prepare to say thanks and to take my leave as she turns to me and says, "Could be a customer, perhaps?"

"A customer?" I reply and immediately seize the opportunity. "I suppose so. Could you have a look?"

"Sure," she replies, and again I'm grateful she doesn't ask me why I want to know. If it were me in her position, I'd be asking.

She clicks away, and then turns her screen towards me. "We have a couple of customers called Weinreich. See." She points at two entries:
- *Weinreich GmbH*
- *Weinreich Holding GmbH*

I look at the two entries. Both based at the same address in Düsseldorf. I quickly memorise the address.

"Are these active customers?" I ask.

Jasmin turns the screen back towards her and clicks away. After a few moments, she turns to look at me. "Yes, both are active customers with Canarus. Weinreich GmbH has an exposure with the bank currently standing at about one million euro and Weinreich Holding of about one point five million."

"Okay, great. You've been fantastic," I say and rise. I'd have tried to get more information, but I've spotted Peter Aulmann through the glass wall that divides the open-plan area and the offices on the other side of the corridor walking towards his office, and I don't want him spotting me and asking what I'm doing here. "Thanks," I say and take my leave, striding towards the door furthest away from where he's heading and take the lift up to see Oliver.

In the lift, I briefly consider my findings. Two entries in the bank's customer base. Is that the

Weinreich the note is referring to? If so, then one minor part of the riddle might be solved. But what does it mean? And what about the second part? *"That's the beginning"* – I'm still totally in the dark regarding that part of the message. And now I'm wondering how I find out more about *"the beginning"* of what?

As I walk towards Oliver's office, I can see through the open door that he's at his desk. I knock and he looks up, smiles at me and beckons me to come in.

"Good morning, Jordan. I wasn't expecting you before nine," he says looking at his watch.

"I couldn't sleep, so decided to come here," I reply, thinking whether I can ask him about the message I received and whether Weinreich has any meaning to him.

"How did you get in?"

"Oh, a friendly employee let me in."

He frowns at that. "That's not allowed," he says. "Who?"

"Didn't ask the name," I say.

"If you're an early riser, I might as well give you a keycard."

"Sure, good idea. Sorry, I don't want anybody getting into trouble," I reply.

He waves that away. "What do you want to see today?"

"Well, having spent the last hours yesterday looking at the credit function, perhaps sales today?"

"Sure, let's do that," he says and picks up his phone.

***

Oliver guides me through seemingly endless corridors and up and down steps and staircases until we reach another open-plan area. Looking through the window I realise we're in a different building. Several desks stand arranged in blocks in the open space separated by partitions. Large plants in big, square pots stand dotted around providing some privacy and break up the large open space. It's a similar setup to the credit team's office area, but here it's a bustling, dynamic atmosphere. Just gone 9 a.m. and already there's the constant ringing of phones and voices of the salespeople talking to their customers and colleagues. I can tell this is his domain. He greets everyone, knows everyone's name and is treated respectfully. I can see he is liked too as we walk through the office space and arrive at a desk where a woman wearing a headset is engrossed in a call. We stop a few steps away, leaving her to conduct her call. Several employees come up to him, and he shakes hands, chats briefly and answers some queries.

The woman terminates her call, looks up and waves cheerily to Oliver.

"This is Sonja," he says to me as we walk over to stand in front of her desk. She rises and shakes my hand. "Sonja, this Jordan Epica. He's from a consultancy we have engaged to do an audit of our systems and processes."

She looks me up and down, but smiles at me and looks back at Oliver.

"Sonja is the team lead of one of the sales teams here. These are the guys and girls that interact with our partners in the retail business. Very busy bees they are too," he says, smiling at Sonja. "Sonja, I'll leave Jordan with you. Please show him everything we do here. Jordan is empowered to look into all aspects. Any questions he has, please provide him with all the info he wants."

He looks at me and smiles. "I'll come pick you up for lunch at around one p.m. Okay?"

I nod a yes, and then he's gone.

Sonja invites me to sit with her at her desk. She's an attractive woman, in her forties with long auburn hair. She's tall, almost as tall as me, and checks me out in a frank manner.

"You don't look like a consultant to me," she says, a teasing smile on her lips.

"Why is that?" I ask, smiling back at her.

"Your hair is too long, your suit is too fashionable and you're too young."

We both enjoy a laugh at that.

"Right, Jordan, what do you want me to show you?" She says it with an undertone of seductive provocation, and in self-defence I start twiddling my wedding ring. It does the trick, and she turns towards her computer screen.

She spends the next hour going through the organisation chart and structure of the business. The sales teams are tasked with supporting the retailers that refer the financing business and recruiting new ones. All the time I sit listening to her, I wonder how I can get her to show me what Weinreich's business is with Canarus. The opportunity arises as she shows me the front-end tool through which retailers generate their referrals.

"So, this is the platform for the retailers," she says as she brings the web-based tool onto the screen. "Each retailer has their own dashboard showing the history of their referrals and the ones currently being processed." She clicks on the buttons bringing up various new screens. Once more it all seems familiar. It's the same kind of thing we had at Hamlays.

"Okay," I say. "It looks very comprehensive. And the referrals they generate go straight through to the credit department?"

"Yes, we have an automated credit-decisioning tool in the back-end that handles about eighty per cent of the incoming referrals."

"I was in the credit department yesterday. I was very impressed," I say. "I was discussing some files with the young lady there, and we ended up discussing a customer called…" I manage a convincing pause, trying to remember the name. "Weinreich, I think it was." I scrutinise her face, trying to see if that triggers a reaction, but it doesn't.

"Weinreich?" she asks.

"Yes, Weinreich GmbH. I assume GmbH is the German term for a limited company?"

"*Ja*," she says, tapping away on her keyboard. "Right, Weinreich. There are two companies by the name of Weinreich. Both based here in Düsseldorf." She spends some time looking at the computer screen. "They are linked together – part of the same group of companies. These are fairly large exposures too, so probably not much that the automated credit process would allow through. They will be handled by a credit underwriter. Let me see…" She taps and clicks some more, before saying, "Yes, the credit underwriter is no one else but our esteemed colleague Peter Aulmann himself."

"Okay," I say, thinking this is interesting information. Judging by her comment, it would seem Peter Aulmann is not that popular here in sales either. "Can you see what the exposure is made up of?"

"Yes." She resumes her high-speed clicking. "We have a lot of IT and office equipment stuff on the books. I would assume that Weinreich Holding, which is the larger of the two exposures, is the parent company. 'Holding' usually implies several subsidiaries, and I would think that they finance all the tech stuff and then lease it out to the subsidiaries. It's common enough."

She clicks on an icon at the top of the screen opening up another program. "Let's see…" she says as she clicks and scrolls through the screens.

"Yes, here," she says, pointing towards the screen. "This is the credit report. Weinreich Holding GmbH seems to be the top group company, there are several operational companies listed, here in Germany and in other countries, and Weinreich GmbH, formerly a machining company, now acts as an intermediate holding company for more operational companies also in Germany and in other countries too. Quite a number in total," she says with a tone of surprise in her voice. Sonja scrolls and clicks some more before stopping and reading out to me. "The shareholder is a company in Switzerland. Not much more on that. Very discrete the Swiss. Oh, and the managing director is a woman: Mrs Elisabeth Schreyer."

I'd love to get a closer look but from the angle I'm looking at the screen, I can't see much. I've been edging closer and now come to realise that Sonja is smiling at me. I have moved too close to her, invading her space. I move back, smiling an apology. Better leave it here for the time being. I decide to embark on a new course, just to avoid arousing any suspicions, and remember the retailer that Jasmin pointed out to me yesterday. The one with the star behind its name.

"Thanks, Sonja, very interesting. So how does this scheme work with the stars? I saw that yesterday too. There was a company called CompuTel IT, and Jasmin told me it was a star retailer."

"Jasmin?" she asks with an undertone I find hard to interpret.

"Yes, Jasmin," I reply, adding, "she was very nice." I say this just to tease her.

A little snort from her confirms my thinking. A small amount of competition going on, it would seem.

"Jasmin explained there's a scheme in place that rewards the retailers based on the business they refer."

"That's correct. It's quite simple really. The more business a retailer refers, the higher their rating. A star rating means a top retailer. They get higher commissions and a bonus at the end of the year based on the amount of business they have referred in the calendar year. They get VIP treatment whenever we meet them in person – for example, at trade fairs or other events."

"Okay, sounds like a good incentive scheme," I reply. "How much commission do they get?"

"Up to four per cent of the financed sum on a single referral."

"And bonus?"

"Anything between one and two per cent of the annual new business volume," Sonja says.

"I suppose that all adds up to a nice sum."

Sonja taps away on her keyboard, scrolls and clicks. "Your retailer, CompuTel IT, earnt about fifty thousand euros last year on commissions and bonus."

"Not bad. Not bad at all," I say as the amount registers in my mind.

"That's the business we're in," she replies.

"And how many retailers work with you?" I ask.

"I guess around four to five hundred on a regular basis."

"Plenty of commissions and bonus—"

"Oh, and by the way," Sonja interrupts me, "your CompuTel IT is the main supplier for Weinreich."

I pause for a moment, startled. I let this information sink in. "Really? Now that's interesting. Well done CompuTel IT." Indeed, an interesting detail.

"Yes, very interesting," Sonja says, "considering they are based in Munich and Weinreich is in Düsseldorf."

This has me almost gaping. An IT company based in Munich supplies a customer in Düsseldorf. Seems just a little bit odd given the distance. Wouldn't one source one's IT closer to home?

"Perhaps they have an office here," I say.

Sonja brings up Google on her screen and enters the company name. She clicks on their website, scrolls and clicks some more. "Doesn't look like it to me," she says after a while.

<h1 style="text-align:center">10</h1>

Oliver takes me across the road and into a small mall that appears to cater to the rich and those aspiring to be seen as rich. There are plenty of classy boutiques, the prices on display exclusive. It's close enough to the Königsallee, Düsseldorf's famous shopping avenue, which is home to the world's famous brands. Incidentally, it is also the city's favourite playground for those who like to pose in their expensive cars and the thousands of tourists who come to watch.

Oliver steers me to a busy Italian restaurant, tucked into a corner on the ground floor and crammed full of businessmen, bankers and the discrete rich, who come to eat lunch and do some shopping. As soon as we enter, the head waiter appears, shakes his hand profusely and leads us to a table at the rear, almost hidden away in a corner. Apparently, it's Oliver's usual table. Oliver and the head waiter talk in Italian, and then the head waiter nods, walks off to return with a bottle of white wine, bottled water and glasses, and sets them out in front of us.

"I hope you don't mind," he says, "but I ordered for us." He sees the expression on my face and laughs. "Don't worry, everything Massimo has on offer is a delight, you'll see."

We sit in silence for a minute, taking in the crowd and the hubbub of conversations going on around us. I observe him out of the corner of my eye, wondering if he might have slipped me the note. But why should he do so?

"Did you have a good morning with Sonja?" he asks after a short while.

"Yes, very interesting. Sonja is quite a character."

Oliver laughs at that last remark. "Yes, she's quite competitive in many ways," he replies, the innuendo clear. "But Sonja and her team are the best in the bank."

"I can imagine," I say, finding myself contemplating if and how I can bring up the topic of Weinreich. And CompuTel IT, for that matter.

Within minutes, Massimo, who it turns out is actually the owner of the establishment, threads his way through to us, nonchalantly negotiating tables and waiting guests. With an easy flourish he sets down two bowls of soup.

"Minestrone," he says with a strong Italian accent.

I try some and Oliver was right, it's a delight. We eat in silence, savouring the soup.

"Oliver, out of interest, what are the settings of the automatic credit tool? I mean, up to what amount will it approve?"

"On a single transaction?"

"Yes," I reply whilst eating my soup. I didn't realise how hungry I was, wolfing the soup down and spooning out the rest, resisting the urge to drink it straight from the bowl.

"Depends, if it's IT or office equipment, then a hundred and fifty thousand euros is the max. If it's assets that have a good value curve, for example machinery or vehicles, it can go up to five hundred thousand on a single transaction."

"And if the company has an existing exposure? Would the system still be able to approve single transactions?"

"That depends on the credit rating of the company. The higher the credit rating, the more the system will allow single transactions to be approved, but there's a ceiling for that. At a certain level of exposure, any transactions that are routed through the system will trigger a manual credit decision. It's effectively like a point on a railway track. You know, activate the point and the train, or perhaps better said the wagons, will be routed off the main track and onto a siding. There they will remain parked until they are evaluated and processed manually."

"Thought so," I say, my glance going from him to Massimo, who has reappeared from the kitchen carrying two enormous bowls with steaming pasta. Whilst he's heading in our direction, the dishes are not for us. He stops two tables short and sets the plates down with what appears to be his customary flourish.

"Why do you ask?"

"Oh, just curious," I answer. But in actual fact, a seed of a thought has established itself in my mind. What if Weinreich's exposure is a scam? What if somebody outside the bank has found a way of manipulating the credit tool? It's been done before. Perhaps the note is a warning that there are odd things going on. However, I'm not willing to share this thought with Oliver for the moment.

We sit and wait for the main course and when Massimo appears once more from the kitchen, I know this time he's heading for us, and I have also decided to spring my question on Oliver. Massimo dances his way over and sets the enormous bowls in front of us. It's spaghetti bolognese, one of my favourites. But I don't linger appreciating the food. My focus is on Oliver, who is spreading out his oversized napkin, tucking an edge into his white shirt. He twirls some of the spaghetti onto his spoon and as he lifts it up, I ask as casual as I can, "Does the name Weinreich mean anything to you?"

He stops halfway, a look of shocked surprise on his face. But I'll give him that much, he recovers quickly.

"No, not specifically," he says, and I can tell he's not telling me the truth. "Why?"

"Oh, just a name that popped up today whilst I was sitting together with Sonja looking at various customers and their files," I say, now busying myself with twirling spaghetti onto my spoon. "A customer connected to a retailer called CompuTel or something like that." I'm getting as good as Alexis at acting innocent, but Oliver is now watching me, trying hard to keep his expression neutral. But it's registered with me that he knows both names: Weinreich and CompuTel IT. Even if he didn't send me the note, he's aware of both companies. It just makes me wonder even more what the hell is going on.

"CompuTel IT," he says, "is a star retailer. They refer a lot of business. One of the best."

"Yes, I saw that," I say, eating my spaghetti but watching him closely. "And what about Weinreich?"

"A familiar name but can't quite place it at the moment," he says. His defensive posture and ambiguity relating to both names make me think there must be a lot more to it. I'm on to something that's for sure. The question is, what precisely am I on to?

We finish the spaghetti. Massimo, who is a very attentive waiter, spots the empty bowls and sidles up to us. "*Contento?*" he asks.

Oliver nods. "*Si.*"

"Tiramisu, panna cotta?"

Oliver goes for the panna cotta, and I select the tiramisu. Massimo nods and strides off with our empty bowls.

We sit, an uneasy silence now between us. Do I push him for more or leave it for the time being? I briefly think of mentioning the note that was slipped under my door but decide to leave it for the time being. If it is him who's behind the note, then he now knows I received it, and then it's down to him to raise the matter. Perhaps he needs more time, who knows? If it wasn't him, then I don't want to appear too pushy. One way or the other, I'm more than intrigued what the note and the matter is all about.

"What are your plans for the afternoon?" Oliver asks as we sip our espressos.

"Oh, I think Sonja still has some input for me." I can sense there's an inner turmoil going on behind those blue eyes of his. I smile at him, trying to convey that whatever it is, and I'm assuming there is something he might want to share, is safe with me. Let him come to me when he's ready. But at the same time my mind is working overdrive, trying to fathom out how I can get to the bottom of the riddle.

11

The taxi threads its way through the heavy evening commuter traffic. The driver starts and stops, the congested roads are bad enough, but the traffic lights seemed to be programmed in such a way as to make the journey last even longer. My driver performs his duty with stoic patience, but then it's okay for him, the meter making the eight-kilometre trip worth his while. After a while, we turn onto a dual carriageway, appropriately named Munich Street, heading south and out of the city centre. We finally pick up speed and within a short period we reach our destination in the southern suburb of Benrath. The driver pulls over at the address I gave him, and I alight at a busy crossroads. I stand on the kerb, taking in my surroundings. There's a tram stop just in front of a seven-eleven styled kiosk on the opposite side of the road, the Schloßallee. I scan the timetable and the route along which it travels through town realising it passes my hotel, albeit underground. At least I will be able to take a cheaper commute back into town.

The address I memorised is right here. Weinreich's registered offices should be exactly where I am. I take a look around, but see no commercial offices large enough to accommodate the space required by a holding company with an international network of companies. Even if run by a small team with purely administrative functions, a holding company like Weinreich would need *some* sizeable office space, I would think. But at first glance nothing suggests that any commercial outfit larger than an insurance agency or accountancy firm has its base here. I walk up and down the road on both sides, looking for the house number. Finally, I find what I'm looking for just around the corner of the kiosk. The corner building, with the kiosk on the ground floor, is the number I need and the entrance to the building is on Kappeler Straße. Apparently, it's primarily a residential building, but on a brass plaque fitted next to the entrance there is the name of a law office and below that another plaque sporting the names of several companies. Halfway down I find Weinreich Holding GmbH and Weinreich GmbH.

I cross back over the Schloßallee to where I stood as I got out of the taxi. I scan the building and on the first floor, directly above the kiosk, I can now make out that there is a suite of offices. Above that, on the second and third floors, are apartments judging by the curtains, flowerpots and shaded lamps standing on the windowsills, and there is furniture visible through the windows. I cross back over the road, walk up Kappeler Straße, looking up to see if there are more offices. But there aren't.

I retrace my steps and almost bump into a young man coming out of the entrance.

"Excuse me," I say, and he stops, turning towards me.

"*Ja?*" he replies.

"I'm looking for a company called Weinreich. There's a plaque here," I say, pointing to the brass plaque next to the entrance. "This seems to be the right address, but there's no bell for them and I can't actually make out if they have an office here."

He turns to look at the plaque, seemingly seeing it for the first time. "I suppose so," he says, "but there's only one commercial enterprise here – the law firm."

"Right, okay," I reply, my suspicions now confirmed. This address is just a shell. A letterbox.

Taking the tram back into town, which halfway along its route becomes an underground train, I ponder my discovery. I do some more research whilst the tram rumbles along on its tracks, but my web search just confirms what I have already worked out. There is no website, nothing at all, and after searching for some minutes I come to the conclusion that both Weinreich companies are just shells. There is no indication at all that they have any operational bases. It all only exists on paper.

***

"How are you, my love?" I ask as I sit on the hard plastic chair at the cheap little formica-topped desk in the stuffy hotel room. The ghastly orange and brown curtains are pulled aside, and I have opened the window wide in the hope of fresher air, but the noise from the street below is too loud. I get up and close the window again.

"I'm okay, Neil," Zuki says, but there's a weariness in her voice.

"Are you sure?"

"Yes, I saw Dr Chang today at the American hospital. He reckons it might be sooner rather than later. You'll need to come home at some point soon, Neil."

Her anxiety worries me, and once more I feel the anger rising inside me that I have to be here on this mission at the same time as Zuki is getting close to giving birth. And I have faith in Dr Chang's opinion. He's proven to be a very good doctor and if he says sooner rather than later, then I believe his judgement. I glance at my watch. It's just a reflex, but I wonder how much time I have left to sort out this stupid riddle and complete Alexis's project.

"I will," I reply.

Dr Chang is Zuki's obstetrician, and in a way I'm glad Zuki insisted, right from the start, on going to the American hospital despite Alexis's assurances that his Cypriot doctors and the hospital in Limassol are just as good. But Zuki wouldn't hear of it. I think it was important to her to have American doctors taking care of her. In any case little Matt, or Jasmine, will be in the best hands and, but this is just incidental, will have US citizenship. Zuki has made sure of that and perhaps, and I'm only guessing here, that's also a reason why Zuki wanted to go to the American hospital from the beginning. Alexis is arranging for our child to have Cypriot citizenship too, but seeing as Zuki is American, and surprisingly doesn't have Cypriot citizenship, and I am a Cypriot only in terms of my fake identity, this is proving a bit difficult. As for me, from a legal perspective, I will be the biological father. No more. Is that enough? I don't know, and I don't want technical details like this to mar the joy of what we are so eagerly expecting. I have pushed all that aside until the time comes to cross that bridge. But it stings me, and I feel the urge to move on with my task here.

"Where's Alexis?" I ask, having failed yet again to reach him. "He's not answering his phone and I need to speak to him."

"I don't know, Neil. I haven't seen him for a couple of days. And Isabelle is in town. I'll ask her when she gets home and let you know."

Zuki sounds tired, so I decide not to bother her with my findings. I'll have to wait until I get hold of Alexis. We ring off, and I sit contemplating my findings. I reach for the pad with the thoughts I jotted down in the early hours of the morning.

Start with Weinreich. That's the beginning.

I can only assume, after what I have been able to find out today, that the "Weinreich" referred to on the note has to do with the companies that Canarus has an exposure with. There's certainly no employee by that name.

On the notepad lying before me I write down:

Fact one: Two companies, linked together, with a shareholder in Switzerland. Letterbox address in Düsseldorf. No operational bases.

Fact two: Both companies have an exposure. Roughly two and a half million in total. IT and office equipment. How come they have an exposure if they only exist on paper?

Fact three: One supplier to both, CompuTel IT – based in Munich. Why Munich?

Fact four: Credit underwriter Peter Aulmann.

Fact five:

I hesitate, thinking. Fact five… But it's not a fact; it's just a hunch. I write <u>*Scam??*</u> I underline the word and question marks.

I look at what I have written. It adds up to sod all.

I get up and pace the room. I open the window wide, hoping once more for some fresher air. I stand at the window, looking out. Despite it being evening now, cars and pedestrians rush by on their way home or on their way into town. Below, a group of young men, boisterous and loud, are heading into the Altstadt and the pubs. Across the road a woman walks by, short blonde hair, sensible shoes, striding along the pavement. The resemblance to Alice is strong, and that seals it for me. I have already been thinking about contacting Alice to help me. I don't have time to spend days sifting through the information and trying to make sense of this riddle. I need answers, and soon. Zuki needs me. Outside help, the help of a professional, is what I need to draw on. I had planned to discuss this with Alexis first, but if he can't be reached, then I will make the decision. Fortunately, I take photos of all the business cards that I'm given and store them in a safe and password app. I find what I'm looking for and hesitate before dialling the number. I should clear this with Alexis. I ring his number once more, but it goes straight to his mailbox. Damn. I decide to send him a text message. I type: *Alexis. Need to talk – urgently!*

I press send and wait a few minutes to see if he answers. Nothing. No call, no reply. Damn him. Where is he?

My mind now made up, I enter Alice's number and feeling nervous, wait for the call to connect. It takes a while, but I hear the clicks as the call is put through. The first thing I hear is a yawn and then the familiar voice is in my ear.

"Alice Jefferson."

"Alice," I say, not sure if I have her attention yet.

"Yes. Who's this?"

"It's me. Jor— Neil Wilson," I correct myself just in time.

"Who?"

"Neil Wilson." And now she's awake.

"Neil… What do I owe the pleasure of this call, at…bloody early in the morning?" I check my watch. Coming up to 8 p.m. here. Where is she?

"I'm sorry, Alice. Shall I call you later on?"

"It is early morning where I am," she says, stifling a yawn. "What's up? You wouldn't be calling me if it wasn't important."

"Ah, yes, but it's not that important that it can't wait a couple of hours," I say, and I can hear faint noises in the background.

"I'm awake now, so cut the shit and shoot," she says, but there's a smile in her voice.

I realise how impulsive I have been. What's the saying? Fools rush in where angels fear to tread. That's me, once more. After all, this lady is ex-NCA or perhaps even NCA again. I don't know. And now I have Alice on the line, waiting for me to tell her what's on my mind. I should have thought this through.

"Alice, I'm sorry. I'm not sure whether this is a good idea…"

"If you're still working for Alexis Theophilou, then it most probably isn't," she says, and I can hear a low chuckle.

I remember a detail from the last time. "You're not recording this are you?"

"Should I be?" I can hear her yawn. "Listen, Neil, you rang me, so you have something on your mind. I'm not NCA anymore, if that's your worry. I'm a freelancer and independent, as I told you. That doesn't mean I'll support criminal activities, but I'm not going to arrest you. I might arrest Alexis, just for fun, but certainly not you." Again, I hear her chuckling.

"Okay, Alice, I'll have to trust you."

"Yep," she says, and I can hear water rushing in the background. What is she doing? I think for a moment, unsure of what to do. I know Alice can help me, she's a forensic analyst after all, and this would be an easy task for her. On the other hand, I haven't cleared this with Alexis, and it's his investment. But so, I argue with myself, I don't have time and I'm doing him a favour by trying to get to the bottom of this little mystery. He'd never approve of me involving an outsider, and certainly not an ex-NCA staff member to boot, but if I can't get hold of him, I'll have to do things my way. Ah well, in for a penny, in for a pound, so I launch into my story.

"Right. Alice, when we last saw each other in January, you said if I need your support I should contact you. Is that offer still standing?"

"Yes, definitely."

"Okay. I am working on a project for my employer. It involves a legitimate investment, and I have stumbled across something that needs clarifying before I can give a recommendation."

"Aha," she says. "I like the emphasis on legitimate." I hear her chuckle.

"Yes, it's a legal and legitimate investment," I stress.

"Okay, and what is it you've stumbled across?"

Bloody hell. There's no way to explain any of this in an indirect way, so I take a deep breath and commit myself.

"It's an investment involving Canarus bank in Germany."

"Canarus?" There's a pause as she digs into her memory. "Isn't that the bank which was involved in a fraud last year?"

"Not a fraud – it was a robbery. A cyber-attack. A digital hit-and-run," I reply, and wait for her reaction.

"Was it now?"

"Yes," I say, knowing full well what it was.

"Okay, well, whatever. And your employer, who I assume to be Alexis, is investing in this bank?"

"Yes."

"I won't ask any details, but if you say it's legitimate, I'll take your word for it."

"Yep, it is. And he doesn't know I'm talking to you."

She laughs. "Neil, what are you getting yourself into?"

"Nothing. I'm buying your services, Alice. That's if you're willing to provide them."

"I'm repeating myself now, Neil. As I told you back in January, I'm freelance now. You employ me, I deliver, and you pay."

"Fine with me, Alice."

"Right, sorted. Now tell me."

I take a deep breath to steady my nerves, get my thoughts into order and focus on what she needs to know. "Alice, as I said I'm here in Düsseldorf, at Canarus bank, conducting an audit for my employer. I'm basically checking if everything is okay as a precondition to my employer providing a loan to the family that owns the bank. It's a substantial loan." I sit down at the desk, placing my notes in front of me. "I have been here two days now, and last evening somebody slipped a note under the door of my hotel room. On this note it says 'Start with Weinreich. That's the beginning'."

"Hold on," she interrupts me. "What was the message?"

"Start with Weinreich. That's the beginning."

"Okay, go on," she says.

"This note, it meant absolutely nothing to me, at first. I've been able to determine that there is no employee with that name working at Canarus. It could be an ex-employee, but I don't think so. I did, however, find out that two of the bank's customers have that name. And they have a combined exposure of about two and a half million euros. Mostly IT and office equipment."

"Okay," she says, and I can picture her, phone clamped to her ear, taking notes.

"The two companies are Weinreich GmbH, which is the equivalent of a limited company, and Weinreich Holding GmbH. Both have a number of subsidiary companies both in Germany and in other countries. What they do I couldn't find out, but apparently Weinreich was originally a machining company."

"Sorry, Neil, how's Weinreich spelt? And where are they based?"

"Right, yes, W-E-I-N-R-E-I-C-H, and they are based here in Düsseldorf. Oh, and the supplier of their IT and office equipment is a company called CompuTel IT, based in Munich, which strikes me as odd seeing that Munich is six hundred kilometres to the south. I'd have thought critical stuff like IT would be sourced closer to home, but that might just be me."

"No, it's a valid point, but I guess IT can be serviced through the web these days."

"Yes, I suppose so," I concede. "What else? Oh yes, the shareholders of Weinreich Holding are based in Switzerland."

"Switzerland?" Alice says, and I can hear her whistle. "Nice and discreet."

"Quite."

I can almost hear her thinking. "And you have no idea who slipped the note under your door?"

"No." I contemplate if I should tell her that I think it's possible Oliver Borrell might have slipped the note, but it seems too abstract. "Canarus is owned by the Borrell family. There's Gunter, the father, mid-sixties, and the patriarch. Then there's Ralph Borrell, the older son, who I think is mid-thirties and a right bastard. And then there's Oliver Borrell, the younger son, early thirties, and who incidentally is the managing director of the business line concerning the referral of IT and office equipment business. It's generated through retailers like CompuTel IT."

"Interesting. Why is Ralph a bastard?"

Shit, I shouldn't have said that. I think for a moment, collecting my thoughts. "He's hostile to us, especially me. I don't know why, but I can't help thinking he's a psychopath."

"A psychopath?"

"Or maybe a sociopath, I don't know."

"That choice of words, Neil, could be significant. What makes you use them?"

"Well…" I hesitate for a moment thinking whether I used the words just superficially, as an insult. But no, I realise I meant it. "Ralph has charm and charisma and according to his brother, Oliver, who is very much in awe of him – perhaps even fear, come to think of it – he's good with the clients, but he came across as hostile, aloof and arrogant. My gut feeling tells me there's something underneath. I think he has his own agenda."

"Agenda concerning what?"

"I can't say, but he – how can I put it? – was totally detached, uninvolved when we had our first meeting with the Borrell family. You know, to discuss the proposition."

"And the proposition was?"

For a moment I wonder if she really needs to know this. After all, it's research on Weinreich and CompuTel IT I want to buy. But I decide to tell her. "The proposition to provide the family with loans. Loans that they need to bolster their capital."

"Loans to the family? And not to the bank? So, the investment is off the books? A private loan to the family? I have to ask, Neil, how big is this loan?"

"Well, they said fifty million euros in total is their requirement. Alex…my employer, is interested in providing a significant portion of the amount, maybe even all of it." Again, I hear a low whistle. "And, yes, off the books. Apparently, the regulators expect the family to inject fresh capital to calm the market and restore trust in the bank following the…the events of last year. Gunter Borrell said they can't raise the capital in the time required."

"The cyber-attack?"

"Yes."

"Okay, two more questions, Neil. Why can't they raise the capital in the time required?"

"According to Gunter, it's tied up."

"Aha. And my second question, what is Ralph's role in the bank?"

"He's the managing director of the private wealth management business. It's prestigious. They look after the fortunes of the very rich."

"The fortunes of the very rich?" she echoes my words. "Hmm… Now that's a good place for a psychopath to be, in a high-level position looking after other people's fortunes." I hear her chuckle. "Okay, Neil, one last thing. What do you think is going on?"

A question I did and at the same time didn't expect. It stuns me into silence for a moment. I have to think hard before I answer. "You know, Alice," I begin, not quite sure of the direction I'm heading. "I can't help but feel there's something clandestine going on. Despite the cyber-attack and the damage it did, for which they were insured by the way, and the regulators putting pressure on the family to inject new capital…well…" And now Alexis's words come rushing back into my head. "I feel that they are rogues."

"Rogues?" Alice says, and I can hear amusement in her voice. "Rogues sounds a very old-fashioned term."

"Miscreants, then. Or scoundrels, villains…frauds, whatever. At the end of the day, criminals."

"Right, let me just think about this for a moment." The line goes quiet. I'm about to ask if she's still there when she says, "Interesting. Send me the details please. Full company names, addresses and a photo of the note. I'll get back to you ASAP. Oh, and by the way, you'd better keep a low profile from now on and don't push too hard to find out any more details for the time being. Whatever this is, it could be dangerous. Especially if, as you say, the older brother is indeed a psychopath."

Alice's words trigger the memory of the mugging attempt. Could it be connected? "Oh, one thing more," I say, almost forgetting my trip to the south of the city. "I went and checked out the address of Weinreich here in Düsseldorf earlier on, but there's nothing there. It's just a letterbox."

"Is that so?" she replies. A moment's pause before she says, "Interesting indeed. But it could mean their corporate offices are elsewhere. It's not uncommon for a company to have their place of business elsewhere than their registered office."

"Yes, but if you google them, there's nothing. Not even a website. Seems odd that a company which doesn't appear to exist should have an exposure of two and a half million."

I hear her take a deep breath. "Yes, does seem a bit odd," she replies.

We end the call, and I lean back in the hard plastic chair. Only now do I notice that I'm sweating. Can I trust Alice? I believe so. I desperately hope so. I have no doubt she's the best there is in her line of work: forensic analysis. If anyone can find out what Weinreich is all about, then she can. And as for her warning, it leaves an uneasy feeling in my stomach. It will be Ralph's area of business I'll be looking at next.

12

I can't believe it's only my third day here, I think to myself as I sprint up the stairs to the main entrance of Canarus bank at 9 a.m. sharp. Oliver is waiting for me just inside the doors. I can tell he's nervous as he smiles a good morning at me. There's no mention of yesterday's lunch and my dropping the name Weinreich into our conversation as he guides me without any deviation over to the private banking department. His demeanour this morning is totally different, and I can't help but wonder if it's the Weinreich topic that has unsettled him or whether it's because we're in his brother's domain that he feels so nervous.

"Heath, this is Jordan," he says to the young man sitting at his desk in the middle of the private banking hall. I can see that Oliver's eyes are focussed on one of the offices situated at the rear end of this part of the hall, reserved for private meetings with the bank's top customers. I glance in the direction he's looking; all the offices are empty. There's an audible sigh of relief and Oliver relaxes a little bit. I return my eyes to the young man who is now standing in front of me.

"Jordan, pleased to meet you," he says in fluent American English.

"Are you American?" I ask, so authentic in his accent.

"No," he replies, laughing, "but I spent a few years in the US. First at uni and then some work experience."

"Could have fooled me," I say, and return his smile. "Heath is not that common a name in Germany, is it?" I ask slightly puzzled.

"No, but my parents greatly admired Heath Ledger, the Australian actor, and named me after him," he replies, smiling his big Americanised smile at me.

Oliver is happy to leave us and within minutes, I realise that he has assigned me to what must be a rising star in the bank. Heath is young, energetic and ambitious. He has neatly styled hair, with a side parting held in place with just the right amount of gel. He's everything I expect a private banker for the rich and famous to be. Immaculately dressed and groomed, with gleaming white teeth, he reminds me of myself when I went up for my job interview with Willem de Vries. But he's definitely more confident, better groomed and much more disciplined.

His job is to look after the private banking clientele and, smiling that American smile, he tells me it boils down to being a nanny. He advises on investments, be it in shares, bonds, and securities. He actively manages his customers' portfolios, buying and selling on their behalf. The ultimate aim is to enhance his customers' wealth. And, incidentally, the bank's. He outlines the various ways the bank makes money from the customer base: commissions and fees from trading on their behalf, selling insurance products and loans. Loans to buy more shares and bonds; loans to buy houses, cars and boats; loans to fund other loans; and very important, so he stresses, to avoid taxes.

Interestingly, he doesn't ask me what I do and why I'm here. He seems to consider me one of the team and doesn't hold back. I get an insight into private banking that is unexpectedly honest and frank. Half of what he does seems to me to be just inside the law. To be worthy of his attention, his customers must have a portfolio of a minimum of one million. Most have a multitude of that. No wonder Ralph likes this business – it's all about egos.

I spend half the day with him, looking and listening. He's good, I have to say. His customers like him and he's a good salesman – on the phone and even better face to face. I watch him preparing pitches, setting up propositions, cajoling and guiding. His eyes are on his monitors, tracking the stock markets around the globe whilst at the same time arranging a loan or giving advice on some tax scheme. By lunchtime, which for this guy is a sandwich and a coffee, he has earnt several thousand euros for the bank. Not bad going for a morning's work.

As we sit at his desk after lunch, I see Ralph striding in. He looks around, obviously looking for me and as he spots me, he comes marching over.

No handshake this time – it's a grunted greeting to Heath and a summons for me to follow him to his office. He walks ahead of me, sits down at his desk and waits for me to take a seat opposite him, the other side of his desk, like an employee.

"Tell me, what is the purpose of this visit of yours, Herr Epica?" No first names now; it's pure hostility.

"What do you mean, *Ralph*?" I deliberately put emphasis on his name.

"I very much object to you snooping around," he says, and I feel a sudden surge of panic rise inside me. Has Oliver warned him that I'm on to Weinreich? I'm aware of the adrenaline now pumping through my system, and with all my strength I maintain a façade of calmness and play totally innocent.

"I have no idea what you mean," I say. "Snooping around?"

"Yes, snooping around. Or whatever you want to call your presence here."

I let out a mental sigh of relief. "Oh, you mean this little audit. Which is something Alexis arranged with your father. And I don't think your father has any objections concerning my visit to ensure the potential investment that Alexis is, in principle, willing to undertake to support your father, and I suppose that includes supporting you, too."

"I don't need your support," he barks, waving me away.

I channel the adrenaline into anger, which I now vent as I lean onto his desk, almost knocking over a red World War One triplane model. "Now listen here, Ralph, whatever issues you might have, I suggest you take them to your father." My delivery is ice cold, of which I feel a short shot of pride, and it has him leaning back in his black leather chair, putting space between himself and my angry face, just inches away. "And I don't give a fuck about what *you* need or don't need. Do I make myself clear?"

He just sits there looking at me. Lost for words, are you? I think to myself. I don't know, but his eyes are like daggers. I stand upright, consciously looking down on him. "Shall we go to your father now, or later?" I say as calmly as I can.

There is no reaction; his eyes are fixed onto me. I suppose that's the thing with bullies. Once they find themselves in a situation where they are bullied themselves, they don't know how to react. I give him a moment. Actually, I even manage to say, "Well?" followed by a couple of seconds for him to say something, before turning and marching out of his office. I even manage to leave the door wide open as I stride away, knowing that I have now made myself an enemy for life.

13

"My dear Mr…er…Jordan," Gunter says, oozing friendliness I know he doesn't feel. Not for me, in any case. For Alexis, I'm sure, he'd be able to put some conviction into it. But I'm just Alexis's employee. Albeit his son-in-law employee, so Alexis had told him, and that makes me more than just an ordinary employee. I'm sure he's given that plenty of consideration, and his conclusion has propelled him to take the initiative. I can see the cogs turning as he thinks about how he can handle this to achieve the best outcome. His incentive, of course, he wants and desperately needs Alexis's money.

"I'm sorry you found Ralph to be somewhat unwelcoming. Nothing personal I can assure you," he says, and I have to restrain myself from laughing. Gunter notices my effort but bravely soldiers on. "Ralph has had a few stressful days and he's just worn out. I apologise once more."

Even though Ralph's and my little conversation occurred yesterday, I'm still feeling fractious. First thing this morning, when I came into the bank, Oliver was hovering by the entrance waiting for me. He escorted me directly here to Gunter's office, albeit

162

with a quick stop en route to have a coffee and to ask me what happened. I told him, and Oliver looked even more nervous.

I watch as Gunter drones on, something about hectic and emotional meetings with demanding customers. He's sitting behind his big shiny black desk, his hair so immaculately styled it looks artificial. I wonder if it's a wig he's wearing.

Gunter's office in the bank is the biggest and the best appointed. It sits in a corner on the top floor of the old bank building, and he has three sides with floor-to-ceiling windows providing a panoramic view across Düsseldorf. It's not as impressive as Willem de Vries' view across London, but it's not bad. That allows just one wall to hang things, and he has one painting on the wall above a long highly polished black sideboard. The painting is massive in its dimensions, covering the complete wall, and the more I look at it the more it appears to have been painted directly onto the wall. I look at it once more out of the corner of my eye. It's impressive not just given the dimensions, but also the vivid colours. Lots of red and yellow and white. I'm surprised because I wouldn't have thought something as modern as this would be Gunter's taste.

"And so, if you agree, we would like to take you out for dinner this evening."

Shit, I lost the frequency halfway through and haven't been listening. I tune back in, hoping I haven't missed anything vital. "Dinner?"

"Yes, if that's agreeable with you?"

"Sure, certainly."

"Wonderful," he says and actually claps his hands. "Is seven p.m. okay with you?"

"Sure," I reply. I get up. "That is an incredible painting, Gunter."

"Yes, my wife had it commissioned. A local painter here in Düsseldorf. Great guy. But to be honest, not quite my taste. A bit fiery for my liking."

Yes, I can see it now, the vivid reds and yellows. Of course, it's flames that are being depicted. His wife giving him hellfire? If she's anything like Ralph, I can imagine her doing just that.

***

True to his word, the big black Mercedes limousine draws up outside the hotel at precisely 7 p.m. I watch for a moment as the driver door opens. I wonder who gets to drive, and am not surprised when Oliver gets out. I move forward, and he smiles at me as he opens the rear door for me to get in. I climb in, sitting next to Gunter. The front passenger seat is free – no Ralph.

"Hello, Jordan," Gunter says and shakes my hand.

Oliver forewarned me to wear something smart but casual, which translates in my case into the same suit and no tie. My suit is beginning to look a bit crumpled, but the hotel doesn't have a valeting service. No surprise really. Gunter has undergone a complete change of dress. He's now wearing a smart blue blazer complete with shiny brass buttons, straight from the yacht club. He's combined this with grey woollen trousers that look shiny new, which come with a crease as sharp as a rapier, and burgundy-coloured loafers. He is bit of a dandy, I must say.

The big Mercedes swings round, and we head out of the Altstadt. Gunter chats away, and I'm wondering where we're heading as Oliver takes some smaller side roads. Before long, we reach our destination: the new port development on the fringe of the Altstadt. Oliver drives up one of the new roads between shiny avant garde office buildings and turns onto a makeshift road, stopping outside a tall, steel and smoked glass structure twenty storeys high. Towering on the edge of this development just where the Rhine bends away and once upon a time the heavily laden barges eased themselves into the commercial harbour to have their goods unloaded. Now it's all shiny new and fancy developments, the homes of media and advertising companies, exclusive designers and consultancy firms.

Whilst Oliver parks the big car in the underground garage, Gunter and I take the lift, a glass and steel one of course, up to the top floor. The doors slide open, and we enter a reception area that appears more like a club rather than just a fancy restaurant. A counter stands in the middle of the open landing, behind it a free-standing living wall with stacks of lilies and other plants. To the sides, smoked glass partitions screen the diners from the guests that stand and wait to be checked in. It looks very exclusive, dimmed lighting, plush carpet, potted plants, and screens covered with silver vine providing discretion and privacy. A young man in a black suit is sitting behind the desk and stands as we walk out of the lift.

"*Guten Abend* – good evening – Herr Borrell," he says with intent formality. "Your table for four is ready."

Another young man, dressed in a black livery, has materialised seemingly from nowhere and escorts us to a table positioned by the glass wall right at the forward corner of the building, facing the Rhine and the entrance to the port. We take our seats, Gunter directing me to sit in the best position, with a prime view of the wide expanse of river, the promenade that leads into the Altstadt and the district of Oberkassel on the other side. I can see Ralph's penthouse from here. It seems a mere stone's throw away.

"That over there, beyond the TV tower – it's 240 metres high by the way – is the parliament building," he says as he points towards another steel and glass building, half hidden behind tall trees on the other side of the port entrance, on the eastern bank of the Rhine. "This used to be the old commercial port," he tells me, "redeveloped in the last twenty years, as you can see. Those buildings there were the initial new development, designed by Frank O. Gehry."

I look in the direction he's pointing and see three oddly shaped structures with curved facades and seemingly leaning out at different angles. One has a brilliant white façade, the middle one a shiny metal façade, the effect like thousands of mirrors reflecting the evening sunlight, and the third a red-bricked façade.

"Nice," I reply. "Very impressive."

"Yes, the media harbour, as it's now called, is a fantastic project, rejuvenating this part of town which has been derelict for many a decade."

Oliver joins us and sits down next to me, leaving the seat next to his father free. He looks at Gunter, who smiles back at him and me.

"Ralph will be here shortly," he says. It sounds more like a wish than a statement.

The waiter appears with heavy leatherbound menus, hands them out and places the last on the place mat in front of the empty seat.

"Drinks?" Gunter asks.

"Sure," I say, waiting to see what Gunter will opt for.

He looks at the waiter and says, "I'll have an Aperol spritz," before turning to me.

"Sounds good, whatever it is. I'll have the same."

"It's an Italian aperitif with Prosecco," Oliver explains. "I'll have just the one, too," he says. "I'm driving," he adds, looking at me.

We turn to study the menus, and I blink as I see there are no prices.

We engage in conversational chat, Gunter expanding on the prestigious redevelopment of the old port, but it soon becomes a bit laboured, and I can see both men glancing at their watches. The drinks are served, and I enjoy the fruity taste of the iced drink.

"This is nice," I say. "I'll have to get some for Alexis."

The conversation dries up. Ralph, I can't help but think, dominates everything, even when he's absent. He is keeping us waiting, much to the growing annoyance of Gunter.

"So, how is your audit coming along?" Gunter asks and just as I'm about to answer, Ralph makes his appearance. I spot his tall figure approaching the table.

"Good evening," he says, smiling at us and in particular at me. Best friends kind of smile. He's put the charm on for this evening, I think as I smile back at him. He sits down next to his father, whose sour look he ignores. Both father and son rest their hands on the table top, and for a moment I see a resemblance between them I hadn't spotted so far. I can't help but notice the oversized signet rings both are sporting. I now know what is engraved on them: RBD for Ralph Borrell-Deselaers and GBD for Gunter Borrell-Deselaers. I find it impossible not to smile at such elitist vanity.

"Von Lettau rang," Ralph says in an apologetic tone looking at me. "And you know how demanding he is," he adds whilst turning to look at his father.

"Ah, yes," Gunter replies, "one of our more demanding clients." This he says addressing me, as if I would know who von Lettau is and just how demanding the bank's clients can be.

"No problem. Clients and bosses always come first," I say, and both Gunter and Ralph laugh at my comment.

The waiter is hovering nearby, and Ralph places his order. "I'll have what everyone else is having."

He turns back to look at me, an easy smile fixed on his face. I study him just for an instant. He certainly has charm, and he is a good-looking man. Wavy black hair, worn fashionably longer, a slight tan, elegantly dressed but not over the top like his father. But it's his eyes that keep me looking at him a little moment too long. The pupils are enlarged, and I can't help but wonder if he's taken something.

Ralph's smile turns into a grin as he sees me scrutinising him, and it's with a physical effort that I pull my eyes away to look at his father, who has asked me a question.

"I'm sorry, Gunter, I didn't catch that."

"The audit?" he repeats. "Are you satisfied with what you have seen so far?"

"Oh sorry, yes," I say, grateful to be able to focus on something else. "So far, yes. What I've seen seems to be all in order," I reply. Of course, I don't mention the note slipped beneath my door and as much as I'd like to, I don't ask who or what Weinreich is all about. I'm sure, though, the answers to that question could be provided by those present here at this table.

"Excellent," Gunter replies. "I trust Alexis is pleased, too," he adds, and I can tell he's expectant of a positive answer from me.

"I haven't spoken to him yet," I reply.

"You haven't?" Gunter asks, but it's more of an exclamation than a question.

"No, I haven't been able to get hold of him."

"Oh," is his reply, coupled with a look of disappointment, which prompts Ralph to laugh.

"I'm sure Jordan will report back to his boss as soon as he can," he says with a little hint of provocation.

"Of course," I say, addressing Ralph. "Clients and bosses always come first."

We eat and drink, and whilst the food and wine are superb, the conversation is forced. Gunter tries his best to keep it flowing, but he soon tires of asking me questions about Cyprus, my role within Stellar Holdings, Alexis's holding company and the various business activities Alexis is involved in, going so far as to suggest some mutual activities. I'm sure if Alexis could hear, he'd be nudging me to explore some of Gunter's proposals, but I don't feel like doing this, not with Ralph and Oliver present. I'd rather leave this to Alexis, so my answers are short and evasive. I see Ralph smiling every time his father attempts to open up a new topic and failing.

After a couple of hours, Gunter gives in, setting his espresso cup down and demonstratively checking his watch. "I'd better get going," he says. "You young men, make the most of this evening. Go somewhere nice, have some cocktails."

I glance from Ralph to Oliver, both nodding their assent. It's all pre-arranged I think to myself. The old man excuses himself, leaving us to move on to where the action is. Male bonding time.

I can see out of the corner of my eye that Oliver is not really keen, but he has his orders. Entertain the man, make him appreciate the hospitality. I'd laugh out loud, it's so foreseeable, but I just smile waiting to see what they have planned.

"Oliver, I'll drive myself home. Take a taxi," Gunter says, and Oliver nods without much enthusiasm.

"You can stay at my place, brother," Ralph chips in, grinning maliciously. "You're always welcome," he says. But nothing seems further than the truth.

***

We cross the bridge to the other side of the port and meander slowly down the promenade towards the old part of town. I can't imagine Ralph frequenting the noisy beer halls, so I wonder where he's going to steer us. Under different circumstances it would be a pleasant evening. The humidity of the last few days has gone and there's a pleasant warm breeze blowing across the Rhine. There's a crowd out, strolling along the promenade or sitting on the high wall that lines the river. Oliver looks forlorn and miserable despite trying to appear otherwise. I'm sure he'd prefer to be anywhere else but here, with his brother. But he's been roped in and has his duty to perform. That's what families are about, I think, knowing very well what thoughts are running round in circles in his head. Ralph talks non-stop, his speech slightly slurred and on automatic. He knocked back a bottle of wine during dinner and several cognacs, much to his father's dismay. His words and sentences come out like machine gun fire, partly incoherent and not making much sense. More and more I get the feeling his behaviour is fuelled not only by alcohol but also by drugs of some sort.

We head past the Altstadt and the beer halls, loud pubs and bars that cater to the boisterous young. At some point we take a right and walk down a narrow side street not much larger than an alley, emerging onto a cobbled street I haven't come across yet. Lined with bars on both sides of the street, the clientele is markedly different to that I have seen in the beer halls. Here the bars cater to students and arty types and, so it would appear, young professionals. It's a mix of characters that is surprising, a mingling of types which seem culturally opposite rather than similar. But the bars are crammed full with young and old, bohemian *and* smart professional. We make our way up the cobbled street, the pavements dense with groups of men and women, drinks in hand, enjoying the warm air. It reminds me somewhat of New Orleans, where I'd once spent a boozy weekend on a stag night during Mardi Gras.

We come to a stop outside a place that is more nightclub than bar. I'm amazed at how busy everywhere is, given it's a Thursday and the time of evening. It's coming up to 11 p.m., last orders in the pubs back in the UK, but here the party is just starting. Ralph walks up to the bouncers guarding the entrance, who greet him respectfully and they instantly let us through a door to the side of the main entrance. We climb some stairs, emerging into a cocktail bar on the first floor. The setting is exclusive; the crowd monied. It's the total opposite to the carnival atmosphere out in the street. The atmosphere is pre-party, the music still turned down and chilled – as chilled as the location itself. The air conditioning is up high, and I feel the coldness of the air on my skin.

Ralph leads the way, stopping every few steps to shake someone's hand or peck the cheek of some pretty girl. It's his regular patch, I think, seeing him mingle with types that look like him, dressed in casual but smart bespoke shirts, designer jeans, designer boots and big expensive watches on their wrists. The women all look the same too: slim bodies dressed in tight dresses or designer jeans, crimson red lipstick on white faces.

Something strikes me as odd about this place; the atmosphere is so metallic and iced it seems quite alien. Definitely not my cup of tea I think, and I laugh out loud – as if one would get a cup of tea in a place like this. I turn to see how Oliver is taking to this place. His smile is fixed and he nods to some people he recognises, but it's not his preferred place or crowd either. I can see by his pained expression he'd rather be at home, with his family, up in the hills where the foxes and hares say goodnight.

Ralph directs us to a long oval booth reserved for us with high-backed seating covered in a red fabric more suited to a lap dancing venue than a cocktail bar. There's a barrier tape separating it from the rest of the crowd with a sign saying "VIPs ONLY". Set along the rear of the club and raised a bit higher than the crowd milling around and watching us with keen eyes, we have a good vantage point to observe the action. I can see there's a dance floor in the middle of the space in front of us, and my assumption is that there'll be a hip and cool DJ later on, spinning his discs, or better said his laptop. Looking at the crowd I can't imagine there'll be ecstatic dancing – more controlled and minimalistic movement to the music. With a crowd as groomed and manicured as this, there won't be any sweat forming. That much is obvious. As soon as we're seated, people start gravitating towards us. Ralph appears to be well known, and he's certainly the centre of attraction for most. I watch him interact. He's charming, attentive, incredibly appealing to the women and cool and confident with the men.

The place begins to fill up, the music is turned up a notch or two and the lighting is progressively dimmed in favour of coloured flashing spots. And the more people who gather around where we are seated, the more seem to be attracted. The barrier tape seems to draw people closer – probably expecting some celebrity and his entourage.

Our oval booth is packed, and I find myself having to slide along the plush red bench to let people sit down. A young waitress keeps up a steady supply of champagne. There are several ice buckets on the table containing champagne bottles. I wonder briefly at the cost of this evening, but apparently the investment is deemed worth it. The waitress takes orders for cocktails and walks over to the bar, only to return with two more bottles of champagne in ice buckets. I watch in awe at the number of orders she is taking and the drinks she is ferrying to our table. I get the impression Ralph is paying for all of it tonight.

A couple of hours pass by, and I'm wondering at which point I can make good my escape without offending my hosts. Whilst sipping from my glass of champagne, I've been watching the people and, most discretely, Ralph.

Ralph was standing close to the booth most of the time, surrounded by his acolytes. At some point he sat down to talk to a pretty blonde woman, and since then he has been making space for others to sit by shifting around on the red sofa. He is now sitting opposite me. I have acknowledged him a couple of times, raised my champagne glass in his direction, but otherwise I've been ignoring him whilst watching him out of the corner of my eye.

I noticed at some point, at least an hour ago, that he looked at me intently before retrieving his phone from his pocket to send a couple of text messages. Since then, several women have appeared who are distinctly unlike the types that encircled our booth before. I have also noticed a couple of men appear too. Men who are not cool and trendy like Ralph's buddies. Their haircuts are too short, and their clothes are off the peg rather than made-to-measure. They are hovering close by but distinctly removed. They are ignoring us with such vigour, which just makes it even more obvious that they are here to observe us.

More champagne arrives, the music gets louder and more persuasive, some in the crowd have even started to move their bodies to the rhythm, and after a while I find myself sandwiched between two young women. Hello, I think, this feels familiar, and my suspicions are confirmed as first one and then the other try to engage in talk and urge me to drink champagne. It's their accents that give them away – distinctly East European – and I am catapulted back in time to that fateful evening of the Holden Industrial Christmas party.

That night I became the victim of a well-rehearsed ploy to get me drunk and drugged. They, and that means Alexis, had it all videoed and used it to coerce me into acquiescing to the inevitable. And it's Ralph's constant looking across at me, no doubt trying to gauge the success of his little scheme, that seals things for me. I refuse the champagne and the attention the two women are trying to bestow on me, which now includes attempts to move closer with hands touching my thighs. I extricate myself from my beleaguered position and make for the toilet.

On my return, I stand at the bar, order a bottled beer and study the barman's every move as he takes a bottle from the fridge, removes the cap and hands the bottle to me. No way am I going to be led down the same path as before. I remember only too well what happened as a result of that night of the Christmas party. And if that's what Ralph is planning, then the game ends here and now.

I see Ralph watching me, and so do the two girls who wave at me to come back over. I ignore them. After a while, Oliver comes over to stand next to me.

"Having a good time?" I ask him.

"Well, it's you that's supposed to be having a good time," he says, shrugging. I can tell he observed what was going on, and I can also tell that he was not surprised by it all. It leaves me to wonder if he knew in advance.

"My good time ends after this beer," I say to him. "But thanks for taking me out and entertaining me."

"Of course. I'll walk you back to your hotel," he replies.

***

We walk through the pedestrian precinct of the Altstadt, dodging the loud groups of inebriated men, the hen and stag parties and the drunk, whose ranks are beginning to grow. Oliver is quiet as we walk side by side, keeping to the edges and steering clear of the intoxicated. I wonder if he's embarrassed, but I don't mention anything or try to engage him in conversation. He has his hands in his trouser pockets, his eyes downcast and I get the feeling that it's the blunt attempt of the two women, no doubt under instructions from Ralph, which are weighing heavy on him.

As we reach the main four-lane thoroughfare and turn right in the direction of my hotel on the other side of the main road, his demeanour changes and I sense some agitation on his side. Perhaps he wants to apologise. Perhaps he wants to tell me something. Perhaps even broach the subject of Weinreich, but I can only guess.

We come to stop at a pedestrian crossing, the light is red for us, and I'm about to turn to him and ask directly what's on his mind, but in that same instant, I become distracted by the sound of a big car engine revving hard further up the road. We both turn to see a black car, perhaps a BMW – I can't tell as it's too dark – with black-tinted windows, its rear twitching as the driver floors the throttle but holds the brakes. I'm about to say, "What a plonker!" when the driver releases the brakes and the car shoots forward. I feel a shove in my back.

I'm propelled out into the road and right into the path of the car. I manage to stop myself from falling, but my forward stumble carries me well out into the road, my arms rotating like propellers to stop that forward motion, my head and eyes turning towards the car.

I watch in horror as I see the car accelerating hard. I even manage to wonder why the driver is not making any effort to step on the brakes. He must be able to see me on the road.

Like in a movie I watch myself as I stand frozen to the spot. My upper body is still in that weird awkward forward movement, my arms rotating madly to stop the momentum driving me further out into the road. I'm unable to move backwards and to the safety of the pavement. I realise in that moment the car is going to hit me. The moment freezes, and I stand like a paralysed animal, staring into the oncoming headlights. I hear the roar of the big engine and the gasps of the people standing at the traffic lights behind me. I hear the beginnings of a scream.

Just then, hands grab the collar and the back cloth of my suit jacket from behind and yank me backwards.

There's surprising strength in the arms that are pulling at me, for I literally fly backwards. I feel something pushing into the small of my back, raising me upwards, and I watch as my feet rise up into the air. My body must be horizontal. I don't know how that can be, but in the same split second as the car should have crushed me, it rushes past, my airborne heels brushing its wing, propelling me sideways.

I crash onto the pavement, landing heavily on my side. I'm winded by the fall, but I manage to look over my shoulder and see Oliver lying on the pavement partly beneath and partly beside me. Only then does my mind register how close that was and how near I came to being struck by that car if it hadn't been for Oliver. He saved me in the very last moment from certain death. I begin to shake, the shock making my nerves and muscles spasm, and I vomit on the pavement.

<h1 style="text-align:center">14</h1>

It's 11 a.m. on Friday morning by the time I get back to the hotel. I'm still in a state of shock, my mind struggling to comprehend the events of last night. I rush to pack my bag, forgetting to change out of my torn and ripped suit, and check out. No way am I staying here. I take a taxi to a hotel near the airport that I book online whilst sitting in the cab. As the taxi cruises through the streets heading towards the airport, I allow my mind to go back over the events *after* the car nearly ended my life. There's a fuzziness in my brain that hasn't cleared yet, but I remember lying on the pavement. I remember seeing Oliver lying on the ground next to me. Next, I remember Oliver back on his feet, his anguish clearly discernible on his face. "Oh my God, oh my God," he kept saying as he then knelt beside me, turning me carefully onto my back and checking me over.

I remember seeing a crowd surrounding us, worried and shocked expressions on the faces of those who stood on the pavement with Oliver and me, and who had shared this experience. And then, as the shock wore off and my brain became stabilised, the memory becomes like a film projected onto the screen of my mind. Grainy and blurred at first, I remember watching as the crowd got bigger, new faces appearing, congregating to see what was going on, their nosy expressions giving them away. In my mind a video is running now, and next I can see the police arriving, two coppers barging their way through the throng, and then the white-clad figures of the ambulance crew. I watch myself lying on the hard, dirty ground, faces all around me. I hear the calls for witnesses and garbled voices exclaiming and shouting out what they saw or didn't see. "A guy with a hoodie!" one bloke yells, but even to me he sounds too drunk to have noticed anything. "There was a guy with a blue jacket – he ran off in that direction!" another shouts. More police arrive, and I watch as they take people aside, noting down details. I observe, as if detached from myself, my body being lifted onto a stretcher and rolled to the waiting ambulance before being driven off to the nearest hospital. I see Oliver in the ambulance beside me, his face distorted and set in a mask of anguish. There's something else there too, but I can't make it out.

And I also recall *my* sudden anguish, lying on the stretcher, a doctor checking me over whilst a paramedic dressed my cuts. The giddy sensation as the ambulance rushed through the streets, its sirens blaring away and the spinning blue lights bouncing off the walls of the houses we pass, making me feel nauseous. A sudden and unexplainable anguish that my true identity will be found out as soon as we reach the hospital. I don't know where that notion sprang from, but I'm convinced that when the doctors examine me, they will see beyond the façade and expose the *real* me: Neil Wilson, fraudster and criminal. I remember struggling with the ambulance crew, and Oliver for that matter, as I tried to get off the stretcher and get away before the façade of Jordan Epica came crumbling down, and my true identity beneath became visible for all to see.

At some point someone shut down my system, and the next I remember is coming round in a hospital bed. Whilst I lay there, slowly resurfacing, I became aware of voices and then, more coherently, of words being spoken in a foreign language. My brain re-engaged with my consciousness and I was finally able to make out what was being said.

"He's been very lucky," a male voice was saying in German. "The car just clipped the heels of his shoes. The force was strong enough to spin him around, but fortunately no damage to the feet other than bruising. But he has been very lucky. No serious damage to other organs, apart from a slight concussion, some bruising and a few cuts. He'll need some crutches for a few days. I understand you were the one who pulled him out of the road. Well done. You saved his life."

The next impression is of the man with the voice leaning over me, checking the reaction of my eyes by blinding me with a torch and talking to me in English.

"Hello there, Mr Epica. Glad to have you back. My name is Doctor Ludwig. Can you hear me?"

There's no point pretending to be asleep with a light being shone into your eyes, so I mumbled in the affirmative.

"You are okay," the doctor says, overemphasising each word as if speaking to a deaf simpleton. "No serious damage done apart from a slight concussion and some bruising. When you get up you will find your heels are severely bruised from where the car hit you, but you will be okay in a short while. Walking will be painful for a couple of days, so we have some crutches for you. Now all you need is rest."

He pats my arm, turns and speaks to Oliver in German. "We will keep him here for a day or two, but he'll be okay. The police will be back to take a statement, perhaps this afternoon or tomorrow." And then he's gone. Next, I see Oliver, leaning over me.

"Jordan, how do you feel?" he asks, his voice tired and troubled.

"Like I came close to being run over," I answer him. "Thanks, Oliver, you saved my bacon."

"Bacon?" he says with a look of bewilderment spreading across his face.

"My life," I answer, smiling at him.

"Oh, you English and your funny words," he says, smiling a very tired smile back at me.

"Doctor says I'll be fine, Oliver. Go home."

"No, I can't leave you here."

"You can. You heard him. I'm not going anywhere," I say. "I'll be fine."

I can tell he's considering my suggestion. He must be worn out; he looks it in any case. He has dark rings under his eyes and his face is pale and gaunt.

"Come on, Oliver, there's nothing more for you to do here. You've been here all night. I'll be fine. Come back later, or better still, I'll call you once I've sorted everything out here."

I can see he's trying to weigh up his options and balance those with his conscience. He's done everything he can for the time being.

"I'm not going anywhere," I repeat. "Not fast in any case," I add as I struggle to sit up and point to the crutches leaning against the hospital bed.

He follows my gaze and laughs. "No, I guess not." He looks at me intently, then makes up his mind. "Okay, Jordan, I'll go home, have a shower and then I'll come back for you."

"You do that, but I'll call you. Get some rest," I say, just wanting him gone so I can think through what to do next.

He stands upright, takes his jacket from the chair by the bed and slips it on. He looks down at me, and I can tell he's as shocked by the events as I am. He nods, his mind made up. "You ring me, Jordan, you hear? When you're ready, you call, and I'll be back to pick you up."

"Will do," I say. I stretch out my hand to him, and after a moment's hesitation, wondering what I'm doing, he takes it. "And thanks, Oliver. I owe you."

"I'm very sorry, Jordan, that this happened."

He closes the door with a soft click, and I sit upright. My feet are bandaged, but the throbbing is audible in my ears. Slowly, I swing my legs over the side and put my feet on the ground. As I try to stand, pain shoots through my heels and I gasp. "Jeez!" I cry out, falling back onto the bed. I reach for the crutches and repeat the process of trying to stand. I have to put the weight on the balls of my feet, but this time round I'm braced for the pain, and it's better. I hobble back and forth trying to gauge if I can walk any distance with the crutches and come to realise that I won't get far. But I have no choice. I need to get out of here and I need to get my stuff from the hotel and get away – fast.

I was willing to consider this as some mad and freaky accident. At first. But then at some point a thought took hold. What if? What if it wasn't an accident? What if it was planned? The car…the shove…

If it was, then I need to get well away from here…and the hotel. And now!

Clumsily I get dressed, my suit torn and ripped, retrieve my wallet, my phone and hotel room key from the drawer in the cabinet next to the bed. Last, I slip my swollen feet into my shoes, wincing with pain as I try to tie the laces. I grab what looks like painkillers and some ointment from the cabinet and supported by the crutches, I hobble over to the door. I open it slowly and look up and down the brightly lit corridor. There's a large hospital trolley parked outside a room further up to the right. I can hear indistinct voices coming from the room.

I look to the left and spot a lift with a sign hanging from the ceiling saying *Ausgang* – exit – and next to it an arrow pointing to the lift. Once more I glance to the right. The voices are still to be heard from within the ward further along. The coast is clear, so, supported by my crutches, I hobble and swing my way down the corridor and press the button.

***

The taxi turns into the circular driveway of the hotel and stops in front of the main doors. I'm grateful that I only need to hobble a short distance to the reception. The driver kindly carries my bag and places it down by my side as I stand at the counter. I tip him generously for his service. I check in as Jordan Epica. What else can I do? I don't have my real passport with me; I left that in Cyprus. The one with my real name: Neil Wilson. Too risky to bring it with me, I'd decided, but just now I could do with it. I wonder if the hospital will inform the police of my disappearance. I assume they will, but it's a risk I'll have to accept. If they do, however, and the police conduct a search for me, then they will find me pretty quickly, especially as my bedraggled appearance raised a few eyebrows down at reception. I explained I'd had an accident, only drawing more attention to myself. If they come asking, not only will they have the booking in the name of Jordan Epica, but also the hotel staff's description.

Now I'm in my room and lying on the box spring bed, a big cushion under my burning heels, do I allow myself to think the whole evening through, with the questions foremost in my mind: Why? *Why should anyone want me dead?* And who? *Who would want me dead?*

For a moment, I allow myself to believe that it might just have been coincidence. Young reckless men in a very powerful car, trying to impress or just showing off. And then, a mad prankster, standing behind me – wearing a dark hoodie or a blue jacket – shoving me out into the road. It's been done, I say to myself, but it's not convincing.

I think back to the beginning of the evening. The dinner, then fast forward to the cocktail bar, and finally the incident at the traffic lights.

Did I miss any vital signs or clues?

The dinner was…was what? Unspectacular. Normal. Sort of, if a dinner with the Borrells can be described as normal. Ralph, eyes oddly out of focus and constantly smiling that cold, menacing smile.

Then the cocktail bar. The women who appeared out of the blue. Hold on, not quite, I now remember. They appeared after Ralph sent some messages. So, it must have been planned.

But for what purpose? What was the goal? Just some paid fun for me? Entertain the lad. Buy him some fun. Make him appreciate the hospitality? No, it didn't have that feel to it. It had a *very* different feel to it.

I now remember Ralph watching me. He was gauging the success of the women's attempts at getting me drunk and my response to their advances. And it might have had a different outcome if I hadn't had the experience of such attentions before. If it was a premeditated attempt to get me into a compromising situation, then I know the motive behind such a scheme: blackmail.

But why should anyone want to blackmail me?

To subdue me? To stop me?

It has to be so. I can't help but feel there's only one reason for it: Weinreich.

It must have something to do with whatever this Weinreich mystery is all about.

And then the incident with the car at the traffic lights. Was that a consequence of the failed scheme in the cocktail bar? My mind drifts back further, to the failed attempt to mug me. If that was the intent. Maybe it was something different altogether.

But again, why?

The answer can only be the same: to intimidate me. Was that the purpose of the mugging? Or to stop me. To stop me from finding out more and jeopardising their plan. Whatever their plan is.

Or, as I think about it, a different angle presents itself: to stop someone else from providing me with more input. If whoever planned this and they reasoned they can't stop the messenger, then an obvious option would be to remove the recipient.

God, this is doing my head in. I try to give my mind a break, but I can't stop churning this conundrum over.

If what I've been pondering is true, and Weinreich is the key to all of this, then the information that is hidden beneath the Weinreich note must be significant. Devastating even. Devastating to whoever is responsible.

And then my mind replays that bit of the film again, the sequence where Ralph gets out his phone, looks at me, looks at the phone, types out his message and looks at me again. And I'm convinced now it must be him who's behind all of this: the failed mugging, the failed attempt in the cocktail bar and, as a consequence, resorting to that other ultimate plan, to have me removed from the game.

But how does he know that I know about Weinreich? Even if, at present, I know nothing in detail. The only people I've mentioned Weinreich to is Jasmin, Sonja and Oliver. One of them must have informed him. But who? Oliver?

The thought makes me shudder. If Ralph was informed of my enquiries and he resorts to such measures to stop me, then the man is a killer. A cold-blooded killer. And now I'm convinced that he *is* a psychopath.

I have one way of finding out, maybe. I check my watch: Friday, 1 p.m. I take out my mobile phone, scroll down to the number I'm looking for and dial.

"Neil." Alice picks up on the first ring.

"Alice, I'm sorry, but believe me, I have good reasons to ask you. Have you found anything out yet?"

"Bloody hell, Neil, you are a pushy customer," she replies, laughter in her voice.

"Alice, I have every reason to be."

"What's up, Neil?" Concern rather than laughter now.

"I'd say there's been an attempt on my life."

"You what?"

"I know it sounds incredible, but I think someone tried to have me knocked over yesterday. Let me summarise it like this: a pedestrian crossing, a car accelerating like mad and a shove in the back. And there I was right in the path of a big black car bearing down on me at breakneck speed."

"Bloody hell, Neil."

"Yes, that's where I'd be if Oliver hadn't pulled me out of the road just in time."

"He saved your life?"

"He did."

"And who pushed you?"

"Good question. Nobody saw anyone apart from sightings of a guy in a hoodie or a blue jacket. Oliver was standing right behind me."

A moment's hesitation. "You reckon he pushed?"

"Alice, I didn't think so at first but now, I have my doubts. My mind has been in a blur – concussion probably. But now, now that I can think straight again, it's possible, isn't it? He might have pushed, and then thought better of it. I don't really see him as a killer. Ralph, yes, but not Oliver. Which leads me to another interesting incident yesterday. I had bit of a confrontational situation with Ralph at the bank, after which Gunter invited me out for an exclusive dinner. A cosy dinner with Gunter, Ralph and Oliver, designed to make amends for the confrontation we had and to build up some bonhomie. Afterwards, it was suggested that we boys go into town to have some drinks together. You know, male bonding activity. Ralph took us to a cocktail bar, where he had reserved a booth. You know, the kind where one sits in a sort of circle, all snug and close to each other.

After a few glasses of champagne, I find myself sitting between two rather pushy and very attentive young ladies. Ring a bell?"

Alice laughs out loud before replying, "Yes, I remember you telling me about such an experience. I take it you disengaged yourself from the lavish attentions and refused the drinks?"

"Yes, I did, and it didn't go unobserved. Ralph's eyes, and Oliver's for that matter, were on me the whole time. And the ladies appeared after Ralph sent a couple of text messages. Oh, and there was an attempt to mug me. Sunday evening."

"An attempt to mug you?"

I hear Alice's words, but I ignore her, needing to finish my train of thought. "I didn't see a connection at first, but now…I think it's all connected. But I don't know how. There's a number of questions I'm asking myself: who and why? And why go from mugging to blackmail to…" And that's when the brutal realisation hits me. I struggle to complete the sentence. The shock and the sheer incredulity of the intent behind these incidents, culminating in the hurtling black car, the roar of its engine etched in my mind, forcing itself upon me. I shudder, and I find myself choking as an uncontrollable sob takes hold of me.

"Murder." Alice completes the sentence. "Neil, where exactly are you?"

I struggle to calm myself. I take a deep breath to steady my nerves. "I'm in a hotel at the airport."

"Okay, good. Have you told anyone else where you are?"

"No, no one. I sent Oliver home; he was with me in the hospital the whole time. And then I cleared out of the hospital, took a taxi to the hotel I was staying in, packed my bags and came here."

"Good. A wise move."

"There's one problem, though. Apart from the fact that the hospital will undoubtedly inform the police that I left without a word, and that means they might be wanting to find out why I left and where I am. I am also limited in my movements. As Oliver pulled me back onto the pavement, the car brushed my heels, and they are badly bruised. I can hardly walk."

"Your heels?"

"Yes, I was airborne, so to say. Oliver yanked me so hard I was sort of horizontal in the air and that's when my heels connected with the car."

"Oh, shit," Alice says, and then the line goes quiet.

"Alice? You still there?"

"Yes, I'm thinking. Your safety is paramount. And yes, the police will probably come looking for you, even if you're not top priority." She lets out a long sigh as she reaches a conclusion. "Neil, you shouldn't be on your own. Ideally, you need to clear out, as in get out of the country. If they resort to such drastic measures, they won't stop now. They'll be looking for you. You should go home. Where's Alexis?"

Now it's my turn to let out a deep sigh. "I have no idea. I haven't been able to get hold of him the whole week…"

Just then, my phone starts vibrating. I hold it a short distance to see who's calling. "Hold on, talk of the devil, he's calling me now. Alice, I'll call you right back, okay?"

As I hold the phone away, my fingers fumbling to connect the call with Alexis, I hear her fading voice say, "Do that, I have info on Weinreich…" I terminate the call.

"Neil, my friend!" he bellows into my ear as the call connects.

"Alexis, where the hell have you been?"

"Neil, I've had a fantastic week. I've met a very clever lady from the Ukraine. Mrs Doctor Oksana Kovalenko. She's a guru when it comes to cryptocurrencies. We need to get into that, Neil. It's fantastic. Full of possibilities—" he enthuses, but I cut him short.

"ALEXIS! Listen to me. Give me a chance to speak!" I shout into the phone.

"Oh," he says and falls silent.

"Alexis, we need to abort the mission here. Immediately."

"Why?"

"There's something going on. And it's escalating. There was an attempt to kill me, yesterday evening."

"What?" he exclaims, his voice loud in my ear.

"Yes, I've stumbled across something. Something that has prompted an attempt to get rid of me."

"What? Why? Are you okay?" he says, worry having replaced the enthusiasm of just a moment ago.

"Yes, I'm okay. Well, sort of, but we'll get to that in a moment. Right, okay, listen. I'll tell you. On Monday evening I received a note. A note pushed under the door of my hotel room. There was a message on it. It said '*Start with Weinreich. That's the beginning*'."

"Who? Wein…? What? Beginning?"

"Just listen, Alexis." He falls silent, and I pick up from where he interrupted me. "*Start with Weinreich. That's the beginning…* That was the message. I had the same reaction as you: who is Weinreich and what is it all about? I tried to get some information, but all I found out was that Canarus has two companies in their customer base with that name. And they are both linked together. But that's as far as I got. But my gut feeling says there's something going on. And it's connected to the Borrells."

"Okay, but how and why is that connected to someone attempting to kill you?"

"That is something I don't know, Alexis. But whatever it is going on beneath the surface, it is critical to someone. That someone doesn't want me to find out or doesn't want whoever it is that slipped me the note to provide more information. Perhaps they don't know who that someone is so decided to remove me. I just don't know. But I'm one hundred per cent certain it has to do with Canarus – and the Borrells."

"Jesus," he says. "And what happened to you?"

"Well, I had a bit of a confrontational situation with Ralph when I got round to looking into his area of responsibility at the bank. He accused me of snooping around. He was very hostile and made it clear he didn't want me there. Gunter tried to placate me by inviting me out to a lavish dinner with Ralph and Oliver, and then suggested that we – Ralph, Oliver and I – should have a few drinks together. You know, male bonding kind of thing. Ralph took us to a fancy cocktail bar and before you know it, there were two ladies either side of me, hands everywhere and urging me to drink champagne with them. Sound familiar to you?"

"Ah, well, I've heard of such things," he replies.

I have to laugh at that and succeed in extracting a chuckle from him.

"In any case, lessons learnt. I extracted myself from that situation and decided to go back to the hotel. Oliver accompanied me. We were standing at a pedestrian crossing waiting to cross when out of the blue this big black car starts accelerating like crazy – you know, full throttle – towards us. As it's hurtling towards us, there's a hard shove in my back and I'm out in the road, a big car bearing down on me. At the last moment, Oliver yanks me back onto the pavement. If he hadn't, I'd be in the morgue."

"Bloody hell," Alexis says, and I can hear the shock in his voice.

"Absolutely."

"But Oliver saved your life?"

"Yes, he did."

"So, it can't be him that tried to…er…get rid of you?"

"I don't know. He might have been the one to shove me. But he might have had second thoughts about it and pulled me back onto the pavement. I don't rank Oliver as a killer. But you never know. Perhaps he was pressured into doing so. There were no witnesses that saw anybody else actually pushing me. There were some wild accusations, a guy with a hoodie or a guy with a blue jacket, but nothing that was substantiated. And he was standing right behind me."

"Hmm, most peculiar, and most alarming. Where are you now?"

"After I scarpered from the hospital, I grabbed my bags and I'm now in a hotel by the airport."

"Hospital?" he asks. "Are you hurt?"

"Slight concussion, bruises, cuts and, worst of all, my heels got bashed as the car sped past. They're severely bruised; I can hardly walk. The hospital gave me crutches."

"Your heels?" he asks, echoing Alice's words and incredulous tone.

"Yes. Oliver yanked me backwards so hard, he pulled me off my feet and I was horizontal in the air. My heels were brushed by the car as it shot past. Enough force of impact to bruise them."

"Bloody hell," he says once more. "Strong man, then."

"Quite. A strong shove and a strong pull."

Alexis is quiet, no doubt thinking about what I've just relayed to him and possible options and next steps.

"We need to get you out of there," he says after a moment. "Can you get on a plane?"

"I suppose so. I don't know whether I'll be able to walk. But the airport will have wheelchairs."

"I'd send Vincent to pick you up, but it will take too long, and anyway he's not here."

"Shame, I could do with him. There's unfinished business here."

"What do you mean?"

"It's not just the car. Sunday evening, two very dodgy-looking characters tried to mug me. I thought at first it was just bad luck that they hit on me. Now I'm not so sure. I think it might well be connected. I'd like to find out what's going on and who's responsible for this. I have a score to settle."

"You what? Mug you? Bloody hell." Alexis falls silent for a moment. "But whatever you do, don't be stupid, Neil. Nothing to be done about all that at the moment. It's unfinished business for them, too. They will undoubtedly be looking for you."

"That's why it would be good if Vincent were able to come here. Where is he? Can't he come?"

"Well—" Alexis sounds a bit sheepish "—he's onboard *Axiom*. I suggested to Oksana that she and her people might enjoy sailing to Athens onboard *Axiom*. They left yesterday morning."

I'm rendered speechless by that piece of information. It's a typical thing for Alexis to do, but it leaves me stranded and vulnerable. Just once, when I could have done with Vincent's muscles, he's sent on a nannying trip.

"Shit," I say, now having to rethink my plans. "Well, at least you now know the situation here," I say. "We abort the mission. Sorry about the investment."

"Ah, now that you mention it," he says, and I feel my stomach begin to churn. "I transferred the money."

"You did what?" I ask.

"Well, you sent that text message. I assumed that was an all clear."

"That was Monday, Alexis, my first day," I say, not believing what my ears are hearing.

There's a long silence and I can hear some atmospheric crackling on the line.

"How much?" I ask after a while.

"Twenty-five," he says, his voice low, dejected and defeated.

"You transferred twenty-five million euros based on a text message?" I say, definitely not believing what my ears are hearing.

"I…" he begins but trails off.

"All the more reason to get to the bottom of this," I say.

"Yeah, but how?"

"Alexis, there's something I have to tell you."

"What now, Neil?"

"I…" I pause momentarily to think how to put this. "I contacted someone to help me investigate the note and to do research on the Weinreich riddle."

"You did what?" he says, his voice going from dejected to alarmed. "Who?"

"Someone I trust."

"Someone you trust? Like whom?"

"Alice," I reply.

"And who the hell is Alice?"

"Alice is ex-NCA. She was one of the agents that came to Cannes."

"You what?" He's back to bellowing. "NCA? As in National Crime Agency?"

"Listen to me, Alexis. Alice is good at her job, very good. She's no longer NCA. She's freelance.

They booted her out of the NCA because of an affair with her boss. She owes them nothing and she won't tell. She can help. And she has information on Weinreich. We should talk to her."

"Are you out of your mind, Neil? You should have asked me first!" he shouts.

"Alexis, I tried a hundred times to contact you. You've been off air the whole week. Apparently entertaining Olga."

"Oksana," he says, his voice back to normal volume.

"Oksana, then. And don't say that I'm out of my mind! I didn't transfer twenty-five million based on a text message."

"All right, all right," he says, all anger dissipated.

"Alexis, we should talk to her. You and me. See what she's found out. And then we can decide what to do, if anything. Worst scenario for you is, you've blown twenty-five million to the wind. Worst scenario for me, I don't manage to get home alive. Then you have that to explain to Zuki." I suddenly realise that Zuki is totally unaware of what's happened to me. For a second, I have to think hard, when did I last speak to her? Jesus, it must have been yesterday morning. "Bloody hell, Zuki. How is she? I haven't spoken to her since yesterday morning. She doesn't know what's happened to me."

"Zuki? She's fine. She's out shopping baby stuff with Isabelle."

15

Lying on the soft and wide box spring bed, I position one of the large pillows under my heels and the other on my lap. I can rest the phone on the pillow without having to hold it the whole time. The hotel room is air conditioned and spacious, and I sigh once more. I have an ice-cold Coke on the little bedside cabinet beside me, taken from the well-stocked minibar. I should have moved to a decent hotel right from the start. Too late now to chide myself over and over again for my stupidity.

It takes me a few frustrating attempts but, in the end, I manage to set up the video conference call on my mobile phone. Alexis struggles to link up, but after a couple of attempts I see him and Alice side by side on the small screen of my smartphone. I have to smile at the images of both of them, the veteran hunter and the evasive predator, so close together on my screen.

"Alice," I say, "I have Alexis on the line. Alexis, can you hear me?"

"Yes," he grumbles, his unwillingness to talk to the ex-agent apparent in his voice and on his face.

"Alexis, I never thought I'd have the pleasure of talking to you in person," Alice says. There's a mix of mockery and humour in her voice and in the expression she shows.

"I'm not sure about the pleasure of it, but I have trust in Neil and if he trusts you, then I am willing to do so, too," Alexis says.

"That's nice to know," she says, grinning.

I quickly intervene before things go off on an unwanted tangent. "Okay, introductions done. Let's get down to business, please. Alice, I have informed Alexis regarding the note. And he's also aware of what's happened."

"Okay," Alice says, her face now serious, and adding quickly before I can get in, "but please let me say the top priority now, Neil, is that you're safe. You should leave the country immediately. In fact, we can have this call anytime."

"I agree," Alexis gets in fast before I can answer.

"I will, but I want to hear what you have to say first, Alice. I have unfinished business here."

"Nothing you will be able to conclude in the state you're in," Alice says with sufficient verve to stop me for a moment.

"Exactly. That's what I've told him, too," interjects Alexis.

"Yes, you're both right," I concede. "But can we just move on. Just for the time being, at least. I'll decide what I'll do afterwards."

"As you like," Alice says, but she's shaking her head in exasperation.

"Alice, the note. Weinreich. You said you had information?"

A loud sigh, but she concedes to my wish. "All right, Neil, all right. I have reason to believe, based on my research, that there's a major scam going on. And Weinreich is the vehicle for it."

I admit, this doesn't surprise me at all. But Alexis of all people is flabbergasted. "A scam?" he exclaims, eyes wide with disbelief. Coming from him it's very humorous.

"Yes, a scam," Alice says, equally surprised by his superfluous display of shock. She knows too well that Alexis is the mastermind behind many a scam. She waits to see if Alexis has anything more to say. He doesn't. "Right, I'll continue then, if I may?" Another pause, just for good measure. "Okay, Weinreich GmbH and Weinreich Holding GmbH and their subsidiary companies are basically non-operative companies. Empty shells. That's corroborated by your findings, Neil. Their address in Düsseldorf is a letterbox address, as you were able to establish. There's no operational base to be found and there's no corporate website. No employees, no profiles on LinkedIn, Facebook or anywhere else. Usually, employees will be active on sites like LinkedIn, or they will talk about their employers on various employer rating platforms, sharing info, or just having a moan. But here there's nothing."

I know all about these techniques. After all, this is how we identified Kerstin, whom we used to trigger Gilbert's deadly software. I had discovered Kerstin on LinkedIn and then followed her to Facebook, where I befriended her and from where I then built up a relationship. Alexis knows all this, but his face is expressionless. He's probably forgotten, considering all things concerning social media are not his domain.

"Oh," Alice continues, "and the managing director of both companies is a lady with the name of Elisabeth Schreyel. I've studied their annual reports and tax documents, and the turnover generated is mainly intracompany. They sell to each other, and they buy from each other. Take the intracompany turnover out and there's basically nothing left. It's a setup I've seen a thousand times. These structures are primarily used to launder money or for VAT scams."

Alexis fortunately keeps shtum at this revelation. I study his face, which he keeps safely tucked behind that expressionless mask. His eyes flicker just once in my direction. We know all about these kinds of setups.

"But the funny thing is, I haven't found any clues that this is what they're actively pursuing," Alice is saying as I tune back in. "Quite the opposite. Using my connections, I was able to do a comprehensive sweep – don't worry, all discrete not to arouse any suspicions or accidentally trigger an alarm," she adds. "And based on the data I was able to gather, I think there must be a totally different motive behind all this." She pauses, letting us digest the information.

"The sole shareholder is a company based in Zurich," she continues, picking up a piece of paper that is lying before her. "The Swiss are, as we all know, very discrete, and it's difficult to get data on companies in Switzerland. But, as I say, I have my connections. And, despite the cleverly constructed shareholding structure, at the end of the day, someone somewhere is registered as economic beneficiary. When it comes to paying tax, the games end." She lets out a short chuckle before carrying on. "But I had to dig deep. And I had to go back quite a bit. You see, irrespective of how cleverly a spider web of companies presents itself today, if you go back far enough, you will find the very first origins – and more often than not, the origins, as in the initial setup, speak volumes.

"And it's no different here. The original Swiss entity was called Düsseldorf Holdings. Düsseldorf a clue? It gets better." As she flicks an errant strand of hair out of her eyes, I can tell Alice is enjoying herself. "Düsseldorf Holdings had two shareholders, again corporates. The first was called GBD Holdings and the second RBD Holdings. And guess who the economic beneficiaries of these two companies were."

"Gunter and Ralph Borrell respectively," I say, the initials from the signet rings springing into my mind.

"Yes," Alice confirms. "But there were some changes over time – name changes and relocations and so forth – all designed to make the current ownership less and less transparent, but the data relevant to the tax authorities only changed once, and now there's only one economic beneficiary left."

"Ralph Borrell," I say.

"Bingo. You're doing well, Neil. Yes, so it is," Alice confirms. "And interestingly, the CEO of this company is also the same lady, Elisabeth Schreyel."

"Who?" Alexis asks.

"Oh, and one more thing," Alice says, ignoring Alexis's question, "the supplier you mentioned, CompuTel IT?"

"Yes?" I ask, knowing in advance what's coming.

"Same thing, except that ultimate shareholder here is a different person. A lady called Johanna Schmidt. Not surprisingly, the managing director is Elisabeth Schreyel. But CompuTel IT is a real company. It's not a shell. In fact, it's a successful company, generating several million in turnover."

"Hold on," Alexis interrupts. "Who's Compu-thingy and who's this Elisabeth person? And Johanna?"

"CompuTel IT is the supplier or retailer that has delivered millions' worth of IT and office equipment stuff to the Weinreich companies," I say.

"On paper…" Alice adds. "It's probably all fake."

"I don't quite get the picture," Alexis says.

"What we have is a cleverly created spider web of companies and a retailer that has supplied millions' worth of non-existent IT and office equipment," I explain. "Ralph is behind all this."

"But who are the ladies you mentioned, Alice?" Alexis asks.

"There's some info on Elisabeth Schreyel. She's real and her credentials and CV seem bona fide. She's registered as residing in Munich and her tax status shows her as single. She's been the managing director of this company – CompuTel IT – for a long time. But Johanna Schmidt, I initially found nothing on her. I then went through the German citizen register and tax database, and was able to establish that she's a housewife and mother. From her tax data, I saw she files a tax return every year for the profits she gets from CompuTel IT, but apart from that there's nothing else. She doesn't seem to work as there are no PAYE declarations, and she has no other corporate shareholdings or significant investments. Based on the tax data, she's either a straw man – or woman – or maybe a puppet installed to disguise the real ownership. Or, and this may also be the case, she's just someone who provided some capital a long time ago to set up the company. It's all a bit foggy." Alice consults her notes. "Oh, she's married to a Peter Aulmann."

"Peter Aulmann?" I gasp at this unexpected piece of information whilst also having to acknowledge with awe the extent of Alice's research. Alice is now focussing on me and despite the small screen, I can see the keenness and intelligence behind those blue eyes. "Peter Aulmann is the head of the credit department within Canarus, and he looks after the Weinreich credit file." I pause as another snippet of information bubbles to the surface in my mind. "And as far as Elisabeth Schreyel is concerned, I think I know who that is."

"Go on then, speak," Alice says after an impatient second's wait.

"I've just remembered a conversation I had with Oliver. He said that Ralph's partner is called Elisabeth."

"There you go – it all adds up nicely," Alice says, grinning.

"But, just a second," Alexis says. "You said earlier on that such structures are usually set up for VAT scams, but then you said you haven't found any signs that this is what they're doing. So, what's the purpose behind all this, then?"

"Yes," Alice replies, "that's a good question. If it were a VAT scam, there'd be loads of transactions, usually small value, across a wide network and preferably spanning the European market. That's the pattern we see in those kinds of setups. But here it seems that the scam is limited to the supply of IT and office equipment. Okay, it adds up to two and a half million, but it doesn't seem to go further than that. And it seems to have stopped." Alice underlines her words with a shrug. "That, indeed, seems stranger than strange."

"Hardly seems worth it, given the risk," Alexis says.

"Worth enough to want to get rid of Neil," Alice says with another shrug of her shoulders.

"He has a point, though, Alice," I say. "Two and a half million is big money, but…well, just not big enough…" I don't finish the sentence. I let my words trail off as I sit thinking. Both Alexis and Alice are watching me. "But on the note, it did say 'That's the beginning'," I add.

"Yes, it did," Alice agrees, and I can see the cogs turning in her head just as they are in mine.

"So there's more," Alexis says, coming to the same conclusion.

"But what?" Alice and I say simultaneously.

There's a long pause as our minds explore possibilities.

"And it still doesn't answer the question of why," Alexis says. "What's the purpose of all this?"

"Only one way to find out," I answer, having made up my mind.

"How?" Alexis asks, and Alice echoes him a split second later.

"Confront Oliver," I say, making it sound simple.

16

Not surprisingly, Alice is all against my plan. I think her precise words were, *"You must be out of your mind!"* And her facial expression matches her words. Alexis at least gives it some consideration.

"With Vincent at your side, I'd say let's do it, but he's miles away from anywhere," he says with a sigh after some minutes thinking and beard stroking.

"Oliver is the weakest link in the whole scheme. And I'm now convinced it was him that sent me the note in the first place," I say.

"Yes, but he's most probably also the one who gave you that shove," Alice says. "He's strong and driven into a corner – you never know what he might do." She raises her hands into the air in a gesture of frustration.

"Yes, agreed. Though I still don't think Oliver is a killer, but you're right," I say, wondering just what any man might do in his situation. "I am convinced that Oliver opposes whatever his brother is up to. Yet he seems to be under a lot of pressure." And another thought has crossed my mind: "I'd also like to know what role Gunter plays in this scheme. I can't imagine that he's not aware of Ralph's machinations."

"True," Alexis says. "And how do they keep this all hushed up? I mean, it's a bank. They have auditors and regulators, don't they? Wouldn't something like this Weinreich scheme and whatever else they might be up to become visible at some point?"

"I don't know. Weinreich might just be flying under the radar, and whatever else they're up to is perhaps still too fresh or even better disguised. It might not be visible to outsiders. That's why I think it's essential that we get to the bottom of this as fast as possible," I say.

Silence descends on the line and both their faces are blank. We're all lost in our thoughts.

"I can come over," Alice says after a moment.

"You what?" Alexis exclaims. "No way. We can't involve you personally in this."

Alice ignores him. "I have an old Europol warrant card. It's not valid, it's not even real, but it has served its purpose in the past," she says, laughing. "It *looks* real, and that might be all it needs to get Oliver to open up."

"That's a high risk to be taking, Alice," I respond, thinking there's much more to Alice Jefferson than I thought possible.

"No, no, no. This is madness, Alice. These people are dangerous. Remember what you said just a few moments ago? *You must be out of your mind!* Your exact words. And why are you willing to risk so much? It's not your concern," Alexis says, alarmed at Alice's proposal.

It's a more than valid question, and I wonder what's driving Alice. It can't be her sense of duty. She's ex-NCA, and Germany is totally out of her jurisdiction even if she were still NCA. And it can't be her sense of justice either, given whom she's talking to.

"Alexis, Neil is determined, can't you tell? He won't stop. He'll do it on his own. And these guys are dangerous. I can't let him do that. I can't sit here knowing he's going to embark on a mission like that and just wish him good luck." She says it matter-of-factly, but still, I find it surprising. "And your man, Vincent, is miles away, as you said yourself."

I know I should be intervening, stopping her from dashing headlong into something that is not her business and might well endanger *her* life as much as mine, but I hesitate, wondering if she really intends on doing this. Plus, she's right. I have already made up my mind.

"Crazy, both of you," Alexis says in desperation. I can see him shaking his head on the small screen.

"It could work," I hear myself saying.

"Oh, bloody hell, Neil," Alexis says, frustration now in his voice. "And what will it achieve?"

"The truth?" I offer. "And I have a score to settle. And maybe a way of getting your money back?"

That shuts him up. For a moment at least. The potential loss of twenty-five million does have some weight, even for him. And if it is a crazy plan that gets him his money back, he'll be fine with it.

Alexis lets out a long sigh of anguish. "Okay. What exactly is your plan?"

"Simple," I say, and for the moment it does sound simple. "Go and see him. At home. A surprise visit. I know where he lives. Maximise the moment of surprise. He doesn't know where I am. They probably assume I've packed my bags and ran to the airport. I've checked out of the hotel they booked, so that's most probably their conclusion."

"And then?" Alexis asks, his face full of disbelief.

"Well, confront him. With the note. And our knowledge of the Weinreich scam. If we get him at home, chances are he'll not get physical. Not with his wife and two small kids as witnesses."

"Okay, but even if you succeed, what comes next?" Alexis can be persistent.

My turn to sigh with despair. "Get to the bottom of it? Get your money back? I don't know. We'll have to play that by ear. If nothing else, blow the whistle on them to the Federal Bank or their auditors, or – last resort – an anonymous tipoff to the police. I'm not letting them get away with it."

"Sure, but just bear in mind, he might go running to Ralph as soon as you leave his house. And Ralph will come after you if what you say about him is true.

And remember, you have a wife here. A wife that is expecting your first child soon."

I hear a sharp intake of breath from Alice and I see her agitated expression. This isn't news to her, but she's probably forgotten. She's about to speak, but I get in before her.

"If so, we get in the car and drive off. And don't stop until we're at the airport here or elsewhere," I reply.

"Crazy…" Alexis mutters, though his resolve at stopping me is dwindling. But he lets off one more shot. "Alice, what's your view on this crazy plan?"

Alice now looks pensive and takes her time to answer. "It's your money, Alexis. And your life, Neil. I'm willing to come over and support you. It won't be muscle I'm providing but back-up and I can be a witness."

"Sorted, then," I say, smiling at them both. Sounds simple, but I feel a tightening in my stomach and the hairs on the back of my neck standing upright.

"Good lord, what will Zuki say?" Alexis mumbles.

"No word to Zuki," I say. The last thing I want is Zuki getting nervous.

Alice clears her throat. "Neil, if you really want to go ahead with this, I'll get on the next available flight to Düsseldorf."

17

It's 10 p.m. by the time there's a knock on the thick hotel room door. Supported by my crutches, I swing across the few metres to the door and check the spyhole. It's her. I open the door and she walks in, a smile on her face but shaking her head.

"You crazy idiot," she says as we try to hug, the crutches in the way, and then she wheels her small travelling case into a corner.

"Alice, how lovely to see you," I say and look her up and down. She looks good. She even has a slight tan, which given her whiter-than-white complexion is a feat. And, as I study her, she still reminds me of Jodie Foster. Her blonde hair is cut to shoulder-length, her face sharp and her eyes keen. She's as I remember her from Cannes.

"Right, pack your stuff. We're moving," she says to me, all business.

"Where to?"

"Two floors down. I booked a room in my name. You have to check out. To all intents and purposes, you have left. Say to the staff that you are leaving, heading home. If anyone comes asking, then that's what reception will remember."

I pack my stuff into my bag, placing it on top of her wheeled case, and together we take the lift down the two floors to the room Alice has booked. Just briefly do I wonder what type of room it will be, but it's an identical room with twin beds rather than one double.

She sees my look and laughs. "Don't worry, Neil. This is strictly business even if we're sharing. And it's purely out of necessity." She takes in the room and checks out the bathroom before going over to the window to pull the blinds closed. "And a question of cost. You'll be reimbursing me for all the expenses." She smiles at me.

"Alexis will be doing that," I answer, smiling too. "I'll go down and check out, then," I say.

"Take my case. It doesn't have to be packed with anything, and it has wheels. That'll make it easier for you. And then leave by the main entrance. Come back in via the underground parking. You can access this floor directly from the garage. I tested that earlier on, after I parked the hire car and checked in. Oh, and let me get the shoes. Size nine."

She unzips her suitcase, upends the contents onto the bed and extracts a pair of sneakers with soft soles. She hands these to me, and I try them on. I walk up and down. They'll do. I'll still need the crutches if I have to go anywhere further than a few steps, but they are soft, springy and my heels feel a lot better in them.

"I'll go as far as the lift but after that, you have to go on your own. Think you can manage?"

"Have to," I say, grabbing the crutches. Alice takes the empty travel case, wheels it to the door and then we set off to the lift.

***

"Done," I say as Alice opens the door upon my return.

"Dropped enough hints that you're leaving?"

"Yes, but I'm sure there are cameras in the underground garage."

"Doesn't matter. It's only if someone comes asking. You're not high priority to the police, but we must assume there's still a possibility that they are looking for you, or maybe someone else for that matter."

We order some snacks and a couple of bottles of wine from room service and sit down at the small table, spreading out our notes, the snacks and pouring wine into the glasses taken from the bathroom.

"Brings back memories of Cannes this does," I say smiling at Alice as we sit together at the table. Alice has placed a pad in front of her, biro lying on top and next to her, in a neat folder, her notes. It's an image of her I remember so vividly from Cannes. I lay my notes out in front of me, ready to formulate our plan.

"A lifetime ago," she replies, but then smiles, too. "That was quite a mission. Cheers."

As we clink glasses, I study her face for a moment, trying to detect signs of bitterness or even anger.

"It's history, Neil," Alice says, catching my look.

"Okay, then down to business."

We sit, going over our notes and discussing the events before turning our focus on to our plan. We try to cover all eventualities: What do we do if that happens? What do we do if that scenario evolves? It's another reminder of our sessions in Cannes, where John wrote down all possible scenarios on flipcharts and stuck them to the walls of the conference room. We don't go as far as that, as there's not that much to plan. It all boils down to springing a surprise visit on Oliver. We decide the best time to strike will be Sunday morning, which gives us one day to kill.

"He might not be at home," Alice comments after reviewing once more what we have scribbled down on the pad.

"Yes, it's a gamble. But it's a risk we just need to live with. Oliver is a family man. I'm sure he'll be at home, enjoying breakfast with his family."

We lean back in our padded chairs, stretching out our legs, our discussion and planning concluded. I check my watch. Nearly 1 a.m.

"Tired?" I ask.

"No, not yet. Too fired up," Alice replies. "Let's finish the bottle and then turn in."

I glance at the bottle, three-quarters full. But I'm too fired up as well for sleep.

"Alice, I know it's none of my business," I say, "but what did happen after we parted in Cannes?"

She glances at me for a second, then scrutinises the wine in her glass before taking a sip. She takes her time answering.

"The question is what happened *in* Cannes," she says after what seems like ages. "I don't know what triggered it, but I should have known it would turn sour. That mission was like being on an adventure. For me at least. I'd never been on a field mission like that before. It had been my idea, and I was elated by the sense of doing something real. All I ever did in the agency was research and analysis. Number crunching and sifting through data. I'm very good at that," she says, looking across at me.

"I know," I say, still impressed with the extent of her research and findings.

"I thought I could achieve something. Something good – for the agency. And I thought too I could help you extricate yourself from the mess you'd got into." She flashes me a smile.

"I was in a tight spot," I answer. Mindful of what I should say, I limit my response.

"And then the setting: Cannes. Summer. Heat. It felt so exotic. I let myself get carried away and John, well, he is, or was, an attractive man. To me at least," she says as she catches my questioning look. "He's a widower. His wife died some years ago. Cancer. My feelings for him were genuine. But I've never been lucky with men. That's why I prefer the company of women." She glances across at me, and it takes me a moment to realise what she's implying.

"Oh," I say. A stupid reaction, but she just chuckles.

"When we got back, he started to avoid me. Relationships within the agency are not encouraged, especially if you're on the same team. I thought he'd come round at some point. I thought his feelings for me were genuine, but they weren't. For him it had been a pleasant distraction. When we were back, he was embarrassed by the implications of our dalliance. He wanted to get back to normal. But I couldn't." She empties her glass in one and pours herself a refill.

"I became a burden to him. All he wanted was for me to carry on in my job. To put it behind me. But that's not how Alice Jefferson functions. I became bolshy, in his eyes. So, he engineered my transfer. He mobbed me out of the team, and I decided to leave." She sits upright and looks me in the eyes. "That's it," she says.

"You said when we met in January, in Limassol, that you…" I struggle to find the right words. "That you made sure… That, well, I was safe… For the time being."

"Oh, that. Yes, I made sure the recordings we had were erased. It didn't seem right to me. A breach of conduct on my side, but I felt they had no right to know. The recordings had been obtained by deceiving you. It was private stuff and none of their business. And I was angry," she says, her eyes cast downwards.

"Hmm…" I reply, not knowing what that actually means. Recordings? I remember her saying the secret app John installed on my phone was able to listen in on everything.

She looks at me, studying my expression. "It means all the recordings are deleted and they don't know about Zuki. But it doesn't mean they don't have intelligence on you, Neil. You are still a fugitive as far as the agency is concerned. They will ignore the fact that you cooperated and that you surrendered the money to us. They will come after you, but for the time being you are not their top priority." She pauses, her eyes now boring into me. "Despite the mission's goal of getting you into Alexis's organisation, you are – in their eyes – a fraudster and potentially a repeat offender. A criminal. Never forget that."

I gulp at this revelation. I desperately try not to think of the cyber-attack on Canarus and the ten million we robbed from them, for fear that Alice might be able to read my mind.

"Talking of criminals," Alice says. "What's it like working for Alexis?"

Bang, there it is. *That* question. A question I should have seen coming. A video stream runs through my mind at high speed: The cyber-attack on Canarus, the multitude of schemes Alexis has running at any given time, and of which I now have knowledge. The VAT scams, the dodgy real estate investments, and the bribes to make things happen the way he wants them to. I try to keep my face expressionless and the alarm out of my voice. "Well, to be honest, so far I haven't come across much that is really incriminating," I say, trying desperately to sound convincing. Judging by Alice's reaction, I'm failing.

"He has a multitude of businesses and an amazing portfolio of investments. He employed me as a general manager in his holding company and from what I've seen so far, it's legitimate stuff, even if there's a bribe or two to move things along. I'm sure that he has *other* activities but so far, he hasn't let me anywhere near them," I lie.

She laughs at me. "Next you're going to tell me that Holden Industrial never happened."

"No, I can't claim that didn't happen," I reply, laughing too. "But with retrospect, it seems so archaic and, now that I know him better, out of character."

"So why did he do it?" Alice asks, the laughter gone and her face earnest.

"I don't really know. Partly I think he did it to get one back on the British establishment and the scorn they poured on him for that, admittedly, silly claim on the heritage. Proclaiming to have family ties to the Holden family. I mean, that was stupid of him, but he had hopes of a title. He wanted a *Sir* to put to his name. Alexis is very emotional and gets carried away with things like that. And I also think he did it to put an end to Willem de Vries' machinations." I say that partly to deflect the direction the conversation has taken and also because I think there's some truth in it. I know now that Alexis is still in contact with Willem, but I have always felt from what Alexis has said that he detested Willem's money-grabbing attitude and the casualness with which he helped himself to money that wasn't his to take.

"Saint Alexis? Is that what you're trying to tell me?" Alice says with some mockery and a slight slur in her voice. "Like his interest in Canarus? Rushing in to provide a loan to the Borrell family to save them and their bank?"

"It's a legitimate investment," I say, noticing with some surprise the defensive tone in my voice.

"No, it's not," Alice replies. "It's a loan designed to exert influence."

I think about her comment for a second. "No, primarily it's a business opportunity. The interest they're willing to pay makes it a sound investment." Of course, I know that's not true. The interest payable on the loan is – or better said, given where we now stand – would have been a positive side effect. Influence and control were the main motives for Alexis.

"Well, anyway, seems this has turned out to be a bad investment." She sighs. "It's none of my business. Not anymore," she says. And I can tell she's unconvinced by what I've told her. "Just remember, Neil, and I've told you this before, crime never pays."

Well, judging by my observations and experience so far, it does. But I keep this to myself.

"Just be careful. It would be a shame to see you behind bars," she says, yawning. "I'm hitting the sack, Neil."

18

Whilst Alice checks out, I stand close to her white Nissan Micra hire car in the shadows of the underground parking. I squeeze myself and the crutches into the tiny car. Using Alice's smartphone as our sat nav, we set off from the hotel, taking the same slip road up to the same motorway I took just a few weeks ago with Alexis and Vincent. It's hard to accept just how different this trip is compared to the one I embarked upon with Alexis just a short time ago. Never would I have dreamt that my original mission would become so distorted.

We drive along the motorway heading east, and I stare out at the same verges, bushes and trees as I did the last time. Now everything has a different feel to it and the anticipation I felt then has changed to dread. We drive in silence, and apart from the directions I need to give, we sit both consumed by our thoughts. It's the very same route that we took as we drove to Gunter's villa. We pass the golf course, the car park densely packed with the same expensive cars and Sunday morning golfers. As we reach Gunter's villa, I slide down low in my seat, a reflex which Alice notices, turning her head to me with a quizzical look.

"That's Gunter's villa," I explain.

She takes her foot off the accelerator, and we coast past the house, both of us looking out of the side window. The house looks deserted, the heavy curtains pulled closed.

"No one at home," Alice comments. "Done a runner maybe?"

We drive past, the morning sun highlighting the golden letters on the wall beneath the roof: *audentes Fortuna iuvat* – fortune favours the bold. It sounds hollow to my ears. "We'll soon find out," I say, hoping indeed that Oliver has not done a runner and our quest will not be in vain.

A few minutes later, the sat nav directs us to take a right, and we turn off the main road and into a quiet residential road. The detached houses here are recently built and stand in large gardens with high walls and even higher bushes, providing security and privacy. We spot the house we're looking for and drive up to it slowly. It is a red-bricked detached house of modern design with a hipped roof covered in glossy black tiles. On all sides we can see tall windows. On the upper floor there are balconies fronted with frameless smoked glass. Like its neighbouring houses it stands secluded, with high walls to the front, facing the road. I spot security cameras mounted on the walls as we drive past at a crawl. A substantial electric steel gate of the sort that slides back on rollers secures the drive. There are a couple of cars parked outside – a sleek black Audi and behind that a people carrier, a Ford or Seat. I can't see which make, but it's of the sort families often opt for. Next to the barrier securing the drive is a separate and equally substantial gate for pedestrians, with an intercom and an integrated camera to see who's standing outside.

We park the car and walk around as unobtrusively as possible trying to get a glimpse of the garden. Through a gap in a hedge at the rear, I can see a large terrace with an assortment of kids' toys and a trampoline on the lawn. But most important I can see lights on in the lounge or dining area.

"Bingo," I say. "Someone's at home."

We return to the car, Alice turning to me in her seat.

"Ready?" she asks.

"Yes." I take a deep breath, scroll through the numbers in my smartphone and hit the call button, switching on the phone's speaker as the call is routed through. It takes a few rings, and I can picture Oliver in my mind looking at the screen in dismay before the call is connected.

"Oliver Borrell," he says into the phone, his voice loud in the confines of the car.

"Oliver, it's me, Jordan." I can see Alice's eyebrows rising in an arc and her face taking on an expression of surprise. Good I remembered, just in time. I concentrate on the call, shutting her out, focussing.

"Jordan, good lord. How are you? And where are you?" To be fair, there's relief in his tone.

"I'm safe, Oliver. That's the most important aspect as far as I'm concerned."

There's a pause on the other end and we can hear kids' voices in the background.

"I'm glad to hear that," he says after a moment.

"We need to talk, Oliver."

Another long pause on his side. "What about?" he replies, his voice guarded.

"I think you know," I reply. "Weinreich."

Another long pause. Shocked into silence this time, maybe.

"You slipped me that note, Oliver," I say.

No reply. "Not over the phone. Not now," he says.

"Then let us in and we'll talk face to face."

"Face to face?" he asks, his voice incredulous.

This is the signal for Alice and me to get out of the car. We cover the few steps to the gate in record time, and I'm thankful for the painkillers numbing the pain. I have the phone pressed to my ear with one hand and the other holding the crutch, supporting me as I hobble across the road. We take up position outside the gate of his house. I can hear him breathing hard through the line.

"Yes, we're outside your house."

"You're what?" he exclaims.

"We're outside your house, Oliver, and we're not leaving. You put the phone down on me and the next thing that'll happen will be the police breaking down your door," I say with enough menace in my voice to convince him.

After a minute the front door to the house opens and a visibly stunned Oliver, dressed in jeans and a polo shirt, stands in the open doorway, the phone still held to his ear.

"I'm not joking, Oliver, now is the time to talk to us," I say and disconnect the call.

Oliver remains immobile, the phone still to his ear, staring at us from the open doorway. Pointing at the gate, I gesture for him to let us in. He twitches, then shakes his body like a dog recovering from a nasty encounter. Alice and I briefly exchange glances as we stand watching him. Finally, he overcomes his shock and reaches to a panel set in the wall.

A buzz as the lock on the gate is mechanically released, and we push open the gate, moving towards him cautiously. Me ahead of Alice, but she's close to me, our eyes trained on him, waiting to see if he attempts to close the door on us. But he doesn't. He just stares at me in disbelief.

As we reach the door, he moves to the side, letting us enter the hall. Inside, we stand looking at each other, his eyes wide, and I can tell he is still paralysed by shock. His wife appears from the dining area, with a look of surprise by this unexpected intrusion. Nobody likes to be disturbed on a Sunday morning.

I turn to face her. "I'm sorry to disturb your breakfast in such a way, Frau Borrell," I say in German to her, having forgotten her first name. "But this is important." I turn back to Oliver.

"What is this all about?" I hear her say, but I ignore her, my eyes on Oliver. Let him manage this situation.

"It's okay, darling," he replies, at last getting over the shock and back into gear. "This is Jordan," he says by way of explanation rather than an introduction. He turns to look at Alice.

"My name is Alice Jefferson," she says in what must have been her best official NCA voice from times past. She says it with authority and holds out her fake Europol warrant card. "I am from Europol. The German police are outside, waiting for us to call them should you not be cooperative," she says, sounding very officious. Oliver glimpses at it, and Alice quickly replaces it in her pocket before he can scrutinise the details. It does the trick, though, and he slumps forward. I take a quick step across, grabbing one arm to support him.

I hear his wife gasp, and she dashes forward to support his other arm. The kids come running up and stop a few feet away looking at their parents with worry. Oliver turns to look at her; his facial expression has changed from shock to guilt.

"Why don't we sit down and talk?" I say, my voice as soothing as I can make it.

He turns his head towards me and nods. I can see now that he's ready to confess.

19

Oliver leads us through to the open lounge next to the dining area. I cast a quick glance around. From what I can see of the ground floor it's a pleasant house – a house lived in by a young family. It's bright and airy, large windows letting in the morning sunlight. The walls are painted in light Mediterranean colours – terracotta browns and light blues. The floors are tiled, no doubt easier to clean with two dynamic children running around. The furniture appears made-to-measure rather than bought in a furniture store and the sofa, into which we sink, is upholstered in leather rather than cloth. The dining room table still bears witness of a breakfast that had just begun, and I can hear Julia, the name having sprung up from the depths of my memory, busying herself now clearing rather than setting out the plates. The kids have been ushered to their rooms, so I assume, for I can hear a TV and laughter from further back in the house.

Oliver sits slumped forward, his head in his hands. Alice glances across at me with a questioning look, but I just nod, a signal to wait. In my experience, people don't like drawn-out silences and will talk just to fill the void. Let him start when he's ready. After

236

a moment he looks up, sees the envelope with my
name on it in one hand and the note in my other. I
don't say a word; I just hold them up for him to see.
He glances in the direction where Julia is busying
herself, and I realise it must be her handwriting on
the envelope.

"I… I…" he stutters, and then manages to
summon up his strength with a long sigh. "I don't
know what to say, Jordan," he begins, his eyes now
fixed on me. "Or where to start."

"The beginning is always the best point to start,"
I reply with a brief smile.

"Yes, the beginning…" he says, his voice trailing
off as he appears to contemplate when exactly the
beginning was.

"Before Weinreich, I would assume," I say as a
prompt.

"Yes, before Weinreich." He takes a deep breath.
"Ralph, as you know, is *different*," he says, and I feel
for him in that moment. It wouldn't be my choice of
word to describe him, but how do you describe
someone like Ralph who, after all, is his brother? "He
is so very ambitious. So very single-minded. He can't
stand losing." He sighs again and takes another deep
breath. Right, I think, here we go.

"He made some very bad judgement calls.
Incurred losses. With money that belonged to our
clients. Rich clients, and very powerful people. He
tried desperately to recover the losses. With some

success at first. But he wouldn't stop. He'd do the same mistakes again and again. My dad, Gunter, went ballistic when he found out."

"And that's when Weinreich came into play?" I ask.

"Not at first. Dad – Gunter – injected cash, the family's cash, at first. Secretly, to cover up the losses. But there was a limit to the cash available. It wasn't enough. So, they had to think of another scheme to generate cash."

"And that's where Weinreich came in?"

"Yes."

"But why didn't Gunter fire him when he found out? Damage control?" I ask.

Oliver snorts a laugh. "Fire Ralph? You must be joking. Ralph is son and heir. He'd never fire him. Me? Yes, but not Ralph. Never."

"Okay, go on," I say.

"Weinreich was an investment my dad and Ralph undertook years ago. Before Ralph started losing money. Weinreich was still an operative company back then. Machining and tools. Old friends of the family, on my mother's side, the Deselaers. Gunter and Ralph, they invested to please my mother. But their combined money couldn't stop the downward slide, and Weinreich ceased trading. Gunter and Ralph held on to the company, paid off the debts, and it just sat there for a time. It was Peter Aulmann who came up with the idea to use Weinreich."

"Peter Aulmann?" I exclaim, not prepared for this revelation. "How come?"

Oliver gives me a long look, perhaps thinking how much I really need to know, but it's too late. He sighs. "Peter's wife, Johanna, and Ralph's partner, Elisabeth, are sisters. Elisabeth told Johanna about Ralph's *problems*, and she went and told Peter."

I look across at Alice, who is sitting there listening and concentrating. For a brief moment I wonder why she's not taking down notes, as I'd expect her to be doing, but then I spot her phone lying on the sofa next to her. She's recording the conversation.

"And the scheme was?" I ask. Lost in thought, it takes a moment before he replies.

"The scheme was to generate funds to compensate the losses by using Weinreich as a vehicle for loans. At first, they submitted small deals for IT and office equipment via the automated credit process. Weinreich, despite the company having stopped trading, still had a credit status that was good enough to get approvals through the automatic scoring system. Small deals, not to arouse any suspicions. Gunter and Ralph started beefing up the balance sheet, generating turnover with fake intracompany deals. Peter made sure no one noticed; he personally controlled the credit process and credit file."

"And CompuTel IT supplied the fake invoices?" I ask.

"Yes, Elisabeth is the managing director of that company. She was able to control the processes and disguise the transactions so nobody noticed."

"But Johanna is the shareholder of CompuTel IT. How does that fit?"

"Johanna effectively loaned Elisabeth the money to set up the company. It was a bona fide investment at the time – it was years ago, after all. Johanna is the sole shareholder, generating earnings through the profits, and Elisabeth manages the company. It was Ralph and Peter who talked both Elisabeth and Johanna into doing it. They thought they were supporting Ralph."

"But what's Peter's interest in such a scheme?"

"Money and control. Control over Ralph. Peter is a manipulative and blackmailing bastard. He wants a position on the board. And he thought supporting Ralph would get him there. Simple."

"Okay, I understand," I say. "But Weinreich has an exposure of two and a half million. How come nobody noticed?"

"It was well disguised. Shareholders in Switzerland. Audited financial statements, bought from accounting firms willing to take a bribe, showing a clean bill of health. And nobody was looking," he says, shrugging.

"So, why did it come to an end?" I ask.

"That cyber-attack last year. All of a sudden everyone was pouring over Canarus's books. The regulators, auditors – everyone. Even Martin."

"Martin Lambeck?" I ask, looking briefly at Alice, who nods to show she recognises the name.

Oliver glances at Alice. "Martin Lambeck is the member of the board responsible for IT. He was appointed to the board after the cyber-attack," he explains, not knowing that Alice has every detail stored in her head. He turns back to me. "Yes, he started going through all the IT-based processes and automatic credit system with a fine-tooth comb looking for potential security gaps. He didn't look into Weinreich, but it became too risky."

"You sent me that note," I say. "Why?"

He halts, taken by surprise at my sudden change of course, his eyes fixed on me. "I can't allow them to get away with it," he says. There's fire in his eyes. "They were covering up Ralph's mistakes. And they were lining their pockets."

"Who was lining their pockets?"

"Peter, mainly. But Johanna and Elisabeth, they too profited."

"And Ralph?"

"No, he's too blind to notice that he's being used. Plus, all he wants is someone to clear up the mess after him."

"And what about Gunter?"

"My father wants to retire with an unblemished record." He lets out a derisive laugh. "He has disengaged himself from that particular scheme. He doesn't want anything to do with it. Not anymore."

I sit looking at Oliver, contemplating his tale so far. "Why did you write 'That's the beginning'?"

Oliver cringes, as if I've given him a blow.

"It didn't stop there," he says after a while.

"It didn't?" I say, puzzled by this new revelation.

"Ralph never stopped. And Weinreich ran dry. He paused for a while but when the regulators and auditors left, he started again. This time it was the bank's money. Proprietary trading."

"You mean he used the bank's money to bet on the markets?" A feeling of dread burns red hot within me.

"Yes. He had successes at first, and that pushed him to go further. But then he started losing money again – big time."

"That's not proprietary trading – that's rogue trading." I sit and think. "And that's why Gunter has been prospecting for capital?"

Oliver has the grace to hang his head in shame. "Yes," he says after a moment's hesitation.

"How much has he lost?"

"I don't know. Millions," he says, his voice barely above a whisper.

"So where is Alexis's money?"

He looks up, anguish on his face. "It's in the bank. It's in an internal account that Gunter has set up. Only he and Ralph have access to it."

"So, all that talk about securing loans to inject fresh capital is a pack of lies. It's to cover up Ralph's trading losses," I say, failing to keep the incredulity out of my voice.

He just nods. I scrutinise his face, and his eyes tell me that he's been powerless to do anything about it.

"From what you have said, it seems Ralph will never stop," I say.

"No," he replies, admitting the truth he himself has had to accept.

"I don't understand Gunter's motive," I say. "Ralph is a loose cannon. Why doesn't he stop him?"

"He can't. Ralph has power over him," Oliver says, frustration and anger now present in his voice.

We sit in silence – Alice and me digesting the information, and Oliver staring into emptiness.

"Why did you shove me into the road?" I ask.

Oliver recoils, shame and even more anguish distorting his features.

"I… I…" he stutters again, tears now welling up in his eyes.

"Why, Oliver?" I repeat my question. "You're not a murderer."

"They put pressure on me," he says in a voice that comes out as a wail, bringing Julia running into the room, a tea towel in her hands. She rushes up to the sofa, stops and looks first down at her husband and then at me, accusingly, as if I've hit him, and then back at Oliver. I ignore her. I want an answer, and I don't care if his wife hears. Oliver looks at me, oblivious to his wife's sudden appearance and her worried expression.

"They said they'd destroy us. Ralph said he'd kill me if I didn't do it. Or worse, he'd kill Julia. Perhaps even the kids. I believed him. There wasn't anything I could do. He had it all planned." He now looks up at his wife and following his gaze, I see the expression on her face change from worry to shame. She knows, I realise.

"You're saying there was nothing you could do?" I exclaim. "You expect me to believe that? So, you decided you'd *murder* me?" I struggle to keep my emotions at bay and suppress the urge to hit him in the face. I keep that safely locked up inside me for the time being, but I'm not done with him yet. I'll settle that score later on.

Oliver crumples, big sobs shaking his body. Julia sits down beside him, placing an arm around his shoulders. She looks at me with a beseeching look on her face. "My husband is a good man, Jordan," she says in a small but imploring voice. "He saved you."

"Indeed, he did," I reply, a crazy laugh escaping nonetheless. "But do you expect me to thank him for it now that the truth is out? He tried to kill me!" I shout.

She averts her eyes and turns to her husband, who sits, head in his hands, his body racked by sobs. I look across at Alice, whose face is blank. But her eyes are burning with anger. I admire her professionalism. So far, she hasn't said a word.

"Ralph didn't know about the note," Oliver continues. "But he saw you as a threat. He screamed at Gunter, blasting him for letting you come over to conduct the audit. He set up that scheme with the women. He wanted to get you drunk – and drugged. And then the plan was to get you into a compromising situation so he could blackmail you into silence. But he saw that the ploy wasn't going to work when you extracted yourself. So, he activated what he called the ultimate solution. The event with the car. He wasn't the driver, but he was in the car. He was livid when he saw me pull you back onto the pavement. He came here, threatening us."

"And the mugging?" I ask.

Oliver looks up at me. "What mugging?"

"On the Sunday evening, my first evening here, two punks attacked me."

"I don't know anything about that," he replies. "Honest to God, I don't," he pleads, and I'm willing to believe him. I let the information sink in, suppressing the tidal waves of anger that keep welling up inside me. I look away, a conscious physical effort in order to stop myself from losing control. The truth is out. Oliver *did* shove me but had second thoughts and pulled me back to safety. Do I thank him for that? "Oliver, we want the money back," I say, turning my eyes back to the heaving heap of misery sitting opposite me.

It takes a while for him to recover. The spasms begin to subside, but the tears are still rolling down his cheeks. He takes the tea towel from his wife, blows his nose and wipes away the tears. Strangely, at that moment, I hear the children crying with laughter from their room whilst at the same time their father sits crying with shame and guilt.

"We want the money back, Oliver," I repeat my demand. My voice is ice. He looks up at me.

"Gunter is away, out of the country," he replies. "There's only Ralph who has access to the account."

"Where is he?" I ask.

"He's at home, I think."

"You think or you know?"

"I know. He's at home today."

"Then we're going there," I say. "And you're coming with us."

Oliver and Julia exchange shocked glances – their faces full of fear.

"But—" Oliver begins to protest, but I don't let him.

"No buts," I say with an authority that crushes his objection. "It's straightforward. We go there and either he returns the money or we will have the police come, and then all of you will be in the shit. It'll be the end of all of you, Oliver, and that includes you and your wife and your children. Do I make myself clear?"

It's a threat I have no idea whether I'll enforce. I don't want the police involved. How would I explain my presence, and my task? And certainly not with my false identity. But my threat succeeds. Oliver looks stricken, and his wife covers up a sob by holding her hand to her mouth and casting her eyes downwards. Oliver realises he has no option. He's gulping down air, and I can see he's desperately trying to think of alternative scenarios but failing. Julia looks traumatised, and I can feel the fear within her. She knows just who the real killer is.

20

Crammed into the little white Nissan Micra, we drive back to Düsseldorf in silence. My mind registered the hard hug Julia gave her husband before we left, dread showing as she said goodbye to him. And I register the concerned look on Alice's face and her silent pleas as she glances repeatedly at me as we drive along. Fear is showing in her eyes, too. But I don't care for their emotions. I have my own. And my emotions verge on committing my own murder.

As we get close to the luxurious apartment block where Ralph looks down on the world from his penthouse fortress, Oliver gives directions, and we manage to find a parking space in a road behind the building.

Supported by my crutch, we walk around to the front of the apartment building and its high-security entrance. I have the crutch not only to support me but also as a potential weapon. The added day's rest yesterday has gone some way in restoring my heels and the double dose of painkillers are doing their bit to suppress the remaining pain. Given what Oliver has said, I have to assume the worst – anything is possible and should it turn nasty, I *will* defend myself.

Oliver falters on the last few steps, and I shove him forward the same way he shoved me into the road, right up to the electronically secured door. A camera is set into the side of the reinforced glass and steel door, so Alice and I keep back, out of the camera's view.

Oliver glances a final time at me, his look pleading.

"Not a word that we're here," I hiss to him, and he nods, reluctantly pressing the doorbell.

The box responds with a tinny metallic ring and after a moment, a slightly distorted but recognisable voice comes through the speaker.

"What do you want?" the voice says, the contempt clearly discernible through the small speaker.

"We need to talk, Ralph," Oliver answers.

"Why?"

Oliver hesitates for a second, wondering what to reply.

"Get us in there," I say in a whisper. "Say the police have been round."

"Because the police have been round."

"The police?" Ralph says, his voice sounding incredulous.

"Yes."

I'm almost at the point of thinking this isn't going to work when an electronic whir releases the catch on the door and Oliver pushes it open. We wait a second before ducking beneath the camera, rushing in after him.

We walk along the short marble-clad corridor to the lift, which arrives as we reach the doors. The lift has a rounded glass front with red LED spotlights in the ceiling, casting a devilish glow. A memory from school days flashes into my mind: Dante's *Inferno* and his journey through the nine circles of hell. The doors open, and I'm half expecting Ralph to step out.

"He's sent it down," Oliver explains as he sees my expression. "Unless you have a key, he has to send it down."

"As long as we can get out without a key, I don't care," I say, and fortunately he nods.

The lift cabin is long and wide, with more small LED spots set into the ceiling providing dim illumination, which suits me.

"This way out when we get to the top?" I ask in a whisper, pointing to the doors of the lift. Oliver nods. I gesture to Alice to get in first, and she moves to the back of the cabin. I follow, keeping as far back from the lift doors and hopefully indistinguishable in the dimness of the rear of the cabin. Oliver stands close to the doors and presses the button for the top floor.

The lift begins its ascent, and I can almost hear my heart thumping. It feels like going into battle or maybe even ascending – rather than descending – into hell.

"How do you want to handle this?" Oliver whispers as we ride up the floors.

"No idea," I say. "Violently if I have to."

The lift slows and stops. The doors slide open. Oliver takes a step forward, like a reluctant soldier coming ashore on a hostile beach. I follow at a faster pace with Alice close behind me.

We emerge onto a wide landing, fanning out. I do a quick three-sixty, taking in as much as I can of the layout but primarily on the lookout for Ralph. But he's nowhere to be seen. Despite the adrenaline pumping through my body, my senses sharpened and focussing on the potential threat of an attack, I manage to acknowledge the impressiveness of the penthouse. We stand on a wide-open landing, floor-to-ceiling windows to the front, providing a panoramic view across the city, the Rhine, and the district of Oberkassel on the opposite side of the broad river.

To our left behind an enormous sliding glass door is a vast roof terrace with teak decking and potted plants. And on the right-hand side of the terrace, I can see a glass-encased bedroom, sliding glass doors providing access to the terrace, and beyond the glass the biggest bed I have ever seen.

I take my time to do a check of the area behind me, slowly spinning around in a full circle. Behind me there are a couple of doors leading to God knows where. The doors are shut, so I focus on the centre of the penthouse and cautiously move forward. This is dominated by an open oval gallery, several metres in diameter, a steel railing running along the entire circumference.

As I move closer, I notice a gap in the railing where a wide, rounded staircase, set to the outside of the open space, leads to the floors below. I briefly glance down and am amazed to see a large model replica of a triplane suspended in mid-air. Its wings are painted red and so is its fuselage. It must be a bespoke replica; I can't imagine something like this can be bought off the shelf. It has been given an aged look, the reds faded with a touch of wear and tear that one would expect on the real thing. I realise it's a World War One fighter plane, and I know enough history to recognise it's the Red Baron's infamous fighter plane. It's big, huge even – its wingspan two to three metres. Its size surprises me the longer I stare at it. It's big enough for a child, or even a teenager, to sit inside. Now I notice the steel cable, fixed to the ceiling in the centre of the open gallery, by which it is suspended at a slight angle, as if banking in flight.

Looking past the plane, down to the ground floor, I can make out an oversized oval glass table with a large vase of flowers standing in the middle. Beyond that I can't make much out, except highly polished wood flooring and the edge of what I can only assume might be a leather recliner. It's quite a drop, I realise – three floors. A neck-breaking height, and

I feel a slight queasiness in my stomach. No wonder there's a sturdy railing to safeguard against any accidents.

I turn back to see what Oliver and Alice are doing. I now notice the numerous oversized framed black and white photos hanging on the walls. Photos of the Red Baron, his plane in various poses and another man, perhaps Jochen Deselaers, the illustrious forebear and close compatriot of the Red Baron. Hanging on the far wall, next to the door that presumably leads into the bedroom, is another oversized framed black and white photo of the Red Baron standing beside his triplane. But the plane has been colourised, its faded red paintwork with the black crosses on a white background in stark contrast to the original black and white photography. The model aircraft hanging in mid-air in the open gallery seems to me to have been created with this photo in mind.

Oliver has gone a few steps in the direction of the roof terrace but has stopped by a closed door. He stands like a cautious soldier wary of potential danger, slightly stooped and listening intently. Alice has moved a few steps to the right, towards the closed doors behind us. She's looking and listening intently in a similar pose as Oliver. And just then I see the door opening, where Oliver is standing, and Ralph steps out from what appears to be a bathroom. His eyes latch onto Oliver first before taking me in. He recognises me, stops dead and his lips curl up into a sneer.

"You." He laughs. "Ha, I've been looking for you everywhere, and now you turn up here with my pathetic brother. How sweet."

He glances briefly at Oliver, his expression switching to contempt. "You fucking pussy," he says, his tone derisive, mocking. He catches Alice's movements, eyes rotating to fix on her. "And who might you be?" he asks in a mock friendly voice, not a bit perturbed by another person standing in his vast penthouse.

"I am the police," Alice says with slightly less authority in her voice than I'd wished for.

Ralph bursts out laughing. He turns to Oliver. "And you were scared of that?" he says, pointing at Alice. Slowly, his eyes turn back to me. He looks me up and down, taking in the crutch under my right arm, and smiles a sinister, evil smile. "So," he says, "isn't this nice. I'd offer you coffee and some biscuits but, to be honest, I don't think I want to. Why are you here, Jordan? Invading my home like a burglar."

He takes slow deliberate steps past Oliver towards me. He laughs as he says, "Look at this. Intruding into my home like a common burglar. No, I'll correct that. A thief. That's more to the truth, isn't it?" Another sneer. "I should call the police. Oh, but I forget, the police are already here." He laughs again. He's coming closer, and I realise my position isn't too favourable, so close to the open gallery and the deep drop down. I move away a few steps, putting some distance between me and the steel railing. "Afraid of heights?" he teases. Another few steps and then he stops. "What do you want?" he shouts, startling us.

"I want Alexis's money back," I say. My voice is hard, as are my emotions, and it doesn't go unnoticed. His facial expression changes, and he turns to look at Oliver.

"I told him everything," Oliver says, defiance and determination making his voice hard, too. "And the police," he adds, gesturing towards Alice. Ralph glances briefly at Alice before turning back to me.

"You bring the police?" he says to me, bewildered. "You of all people bring the police? Don't you think that's a bit *ironic*?" He laughs out loud and turns to his brother. "Have you still not realised who this is?"

Oliver switches his eyes from Ralph to me, a questioning frown forming on his face. I hold my breath, wondering what Ralph's going to say next. Surely, he can't know it was me behind the cyber-attack last November.

"This, my dear brother, is the man that robbed his own employer," Ralph says triumphantly. "Despite his new name, Jordan Epica, and how pathetic a name that is, this is actually Neil Wilson. Neil and his father-in-law, that was good by the way, Alexis

Theophilou, robbed Hamlays Bank, Neil's employer at the time, of twenty-five million." Ralph winks at me, and I sigh inwardly with relief that it's not the cyber-attack on Canarus he's referring to. But still I wonder how he found out about Hamlays, and it obviously shows on my face, for he laughs at my expression.

"You're wondering how I know, eh? You're not the only one with connections, Jordan – or should I call you Neil?" He sniggers. "Willem is a good friend of the family."

I admit to being perplexed by this revelation. I can't believe Willem would speak about that episode, especially as he was involved himself, taking a million or two in handouts for his part in defrauding Hamlays – and according to Alexis's version of the truth, the instigator behind numerous other frauds and schemes that cost the bank millions.

"How funny, eh, Neil?" Ralph chuckles. "But which makes me wonder," he says, now turning to Alice, "just who the fuck are you?"

Both Oliver and I turn our heads to look at Alice.

"I'm Alice Jefferson, Europol officer and National Crime Agency UK. And Neil was and is an undercover agent for the NCA."

"Is he now?" Ralph says, turning his face and eyes back on me, accompanied by another eerie chuckle. I wonder once more if he's on drugs. He takes two quick menacing steps closer to me. I shuffle two steps to the side, keeping the distance between us. Ralph smiles at my reflex.

"Mr Borrell – Ralph – that's enough!" Alice commands, taking several determined steps towards us. But her resolve falters and she stops, her determination gone.

Ralph hears Alice's words but ignores her. And then he grins at me. "Okay, so now get the fuck out of my house!" he shouts.

"Not without Alexis's money," I say, standing my ground.

"The twenty-five he stole? A thief, just like you," Ralph says, laughing and raising his arms and hands into the air – a gesture meant to emphasise the ludicrousness of my demand.

I'm watching him closely. His hands and arms are still up in the air, but he's balling his hands into fists. A stance that signals a potential move on his side. I shuffle sideways, trying to put myself in a less prone position. He watches me, following my moves. I can make out a slight tic in his right eye and his facial expression has tensed. The release of adrenaline switches to turbo mode as my mind acknowledges the imminent threat.

With a low growl, Ralph lunges at me. It's a kamikaze thrust, his intention to propel me, and maybe us both, over the railing. But he's misjudged the gap between us, giving me the time to shove my crutch between his feet. He trips and begins to fall, the force and direction of his thrust deflected just far enough for me to grab his right arm with both my hands. I channel all my hate, my anguish and all my fear into that movement and pull him forward, propelling him over the railing and into the void behind me.

Time seems to stop. For an infinitesimal fraction of a second there's nothing. And then there's a crash below. The sickening thump of the impact of his body and the shattering of glass. And then silence again.

Into the silence, I hear myself breathe out. I turn to look. Down below, lying on top of his smashed red warplane, torn from its steel anchor in the ceiling above and surrounded by broken glass, Ralph lies motionless. Blood forms a growing pool by his head, much darker than the colour of the Red Baron's smashed plane. I stare at the body and the pool of blood slowly spreading.

Alice rushes to my side, looks down and gasps. She turns to hold Oliver back, but he pushes to get past her, grabs the railing and despite her best efforts to keep him away, he pulls himself forward and looks down at the broken, lifeless body of his brother. He doesn't gasp; he doesn't cry out. He just sighs. A very long sigh – perhaps the release of many decades' worth of pent-up anguish, fear or loathing. I don't know, but that sigh burns itself into my memory.

All of a sudden Alice appears down below and takes a tentative step onto the shards of glass. My mind ponders how she got down there so fast. She must have flown. I suppress a giggle.

She kneels down and feels for a pulse. She looks up, shaking her head.

I summon my strength and force myself to think and act. I take the staircase down, slowly, step by step, like walking down a red-carpeted staircase to meet guests at a function. It seems to take ages. As I reach the bottom, my eyes take in the vast living area, the white leather sofa, as big as an island, facing the wall of glass and the exquisite view across the Rhine, the incredibly large TV screen, the bar in the corner and two leather recliners with another glass table standing between them. I think to myself why does it always have to be glass and chrome and oversized? But it doesn't really register. I stop a few feet away from the carnage. I look at Ralph, who's lying face down across the wreckage of the Red Baron's triplane.

My eyes settle on his head. How strange, there's something sticking out of the back of his head. Is that a metal rod? Red and something else is dripping from the metal onto his shoulders. Mesmerised, I stand and look. How odd that the triplane disintegrated like that. It must have been made of paper, I think. Paper and soft wood and metal rods. Flying kites, isn't that what they called them? Alice is moving around the debris, crouching, rising, only to crouch down again. What the hell is she doing?

Oliver appears beside me. He, too, looks at the debris, his eyes finally fixing on the gory mess. He starts to heave, turns and dashes away. "Pussy," I say, chuckling, watching his speedy departure, and I have no idea why I said it. I turn my head back surprised to find Alice standing right in front of me. She has a fiery look in her eyes, and I begin to snigger. I'm stopped short by a hard right-hander across my face. The effect is like submerging your head in a barrel of ice-cold water – sobering.

"Neil, for fuck's sake, get a grip," she hisses at me.

"Jeez," I splutter, but I'm back in the here and now. "We need to get out of here," I say.

"We need to call the police," Alice says.

"No way," I say. "We get the hell out of here."

I take a look around, my mind in turmoil. She's right, the decent thing would be to call the police. But how do you explain all this? My eyes flit back and forth. I see more framed black and white photos on the walls, and smaller models of World War planes standing on sideboards and placed within a tall bookshelf that covers a whole wall at the back. "God, he's obsessed with the bloody things," I say to myself, unaware that I'm speaking out loud. I spot a small desk standing in one of the few corners. Another bloody glass and chrome thing, but it's the sight of the laptop on the desk that triggers me. The lid is open and there's a recurring blink of a small LED. It's on. I walk over to it and press the return button. The screen comes to life, a screensaver showing on the monitor.

Oliver stumbles back in, pale and with his hand to his mouth.

"Oliver," I say, pointing to the computer. He looks at it and shrugs. "Come on, man, get a grip. It's on. What's the access code?"

I hear Alice say, "Neil, leave him…" But I ignore her. I'm not leaving without trying.

"Oliver, I know you damn well know. Now get to it." There's no doubt in my mind that Oliver knows more than he's willing to let on. And I'm beginning to feel the murderous anger rise again within me.

I think Oliver senses it too, for he gives me a long look and then walks over to the desk. Leaning over, he enters something and presses return.

I move across and stand beside him. "Can you enter the bank's systems?"

He doesn't reply, but uses the touchpad to steer the cursor onto an icon and then double taps it. The screen is filled with a login page, the Canarus logo in the top right corner.

"Do it," I command. Oliver bends down, enters Ralph's login details and presses enter. "What's this?" I ask, expecting an online banking interface.

"It's the bank's back-end system," he says.

"Is this where one accesses the internal accounts?"

"Yes," he says, and turns to look at me.

"Can you access the account where Alexis's money is deposited?"

"Yes, but I don't have the passkey to the account."

"Shit," I say. So close but still so far.

Alice appears by my side and looks down at the screen. "How's the passkey configured? Letters, numbers?"

"Yes, it's a combination of letters, numbers and characters," Oliver replies.

"Show me," I say, and Oliver navigates through the system, bringing up the internal account on the screen. A prompt is flashing on the access screen.

"How many letters, numbers and characters?"

"A minimum of twelve."

"And you have no idea what it could be?"

"No," he says, and judging by the look on his face, he doesn't.

"Fuck!" I exclaim.

Alice speaks up, "Is it random or can you use a pattern? You know like 'Alice5000!'"

"Well, it's a combination but yes, you can use a pattern like that," Oliver replies after some thought.

"Okay," I say, hope returning. "Does Ralph have a pattern?"

"I don't really know," he replies.

"Oliver, for fuck's sake," I almost scream at him. "Think!" I'm aware of time flying by and I'm beginning to get nervous. The longer we stay here, the higher the risk somebody might come. Perhaps. Or maybe not. I don't know. But I just want to get away from here.

"I don't know!" he wails.

"Come on, Oliver. You must have an idea. He's your brother. You've been working side by side for years."

"Well, he used patterns, but it was always changing, depending on his interests."

"His interests?" I say.

"Well, he was into Jaguar cars for a while, so he used 'Jag' followed by his initials and his date of birth. And then he'd change it."

"So maybe something like that, then. What are his initials?" Alice asks.

"RBD," Oliver and I say simultaneously.

"Shit, it could be anything," Alice says, resignation in her voice.

"Jeez!" I bellow in frustration, grabbing a chrome paperweight from the desk and throwing it across the room, having momentarily forgotten the carnage behind me. Luckily, it doesn't hit the prostrate form of Ralph lying on his destroyed model plane. It hits the floor just in front of the wreck. But it gives me a thought. "I have an app on my phone where I store all my passwords."

"So do I," Alice echoes, picking up on my train of thought.

"Yes, me too," Oliver says.

"Would Ralph have something like that?" I fix my eyes on Oliver, scrutinising his reaction. If he tries to lie, I'll spot it.

"Probably," he says, and I can see he's thinking hard, trying to remember. "Yes, he does have an app like that on his phone."

"Okay, where is it?"

We begin a search that takes us up and down the three floors of his penthouse. Oliver checks his bedroom, Alice explores the various rooms one floor up and I search the ground floor. As we return empty-handed to our starting point, the desk, we concede that there's one place we haven't searched: his body. With trepidation we move across to the bloody mess with the prone figure lying atop the crushed debris of the plane. Ralph is lying face down, and in the right back pocket of his jeans I spot the shape of a smartphone. Same place I put mine, I think.

Averting my eyes from the sight of the blood and gore, I bend down to retrieve the phone, gagging on the metallic smell that creeps up my nostrils.

"Hold it," Alice commands, and I look up questioningly. "Gloves. Got to find some gloves first."

"Gloves?" I ask, at first not understanding why she wants gloves. But then I realise – fingerprints.

"Maybe in the kitchen," I say to her.

"Or in the utility room over there," Oliver says, but he doesn't move. He seems stuck to the floor.

Alice dashes over to the open kitchen area, pulling out drawers and opening the doors of each unit. Finding nothing, she rushes over to the utility room, returning with rubber gloves with bleach stains on them.

I squeeze my hands into them and prise the phone from his pocket. Holding up the phone like something acidic, we return to the desk, where I lie it down. It's an iPhone, the latest model. I press the button on the side and the screen comes to life.

"Touch ID," I say as we all stand looking down at it. I give an involuntary shudder thinking that to access this we need a fingerprint. "Oh God," I groan. It escapes my mouth, I can't help it, and we turn in unison to look at Ralph's body.

As I'm the one wearing the gloves, the gruesome task is mine to go over and get the fingerprint. This time I go alone, the other two staying put, united in their reluctance to get that close to the body and perform the task.

I take a deep breath as I walk over to Ralph's body. I go down on my knees, brushing away the broken glass. This close, the metallic smell is overpowering. I avert my eyes from the grisly sight of the pool of blood and, even worse, the gore surrounding the wound and sticking to the metal rod.

Gingerly, I take hold of his right hand, stretch out the index finger and hold it against the phone's screen. Then the bloody phone slips from my grasp, the cumbersome rubber gloves not providing enough grip. I clench my teeth as I steel myself to repeat the process. With a big sigh of relief, I watch as the touch ID screen disappears, and I stand up looking at the welcome screen and a photo of a very attractive blonde woman, windswept hair partly obscuring her eyes, smiling at the camera. It must be Elisabeth, I surmise, and I finally get to see the face of the woman who has been so instrumental in orchestrating this deception.

I walk back over to the desk, place down the phone and spot a touchscreen pen in a chrome penholder. I take it and press it against the screen. I don't want it to time out, forcing me to repeat the gruesome task once more.

"We need to find the app," I say, looking at Oliver.

"I can't see properly," he says and looks around. He sees a dishcloth and walks over to fetch it. "Give me the phone," he says, and I hand it over. He takes the phone with the dishcloth and then with his other hand the pen. "It's okay," he says as he sees my expression. "My fingerprints are all over this place, but not on his phone and as far as this pen is concerned, well, it's mine now."

He uses the pen to scroll through the screens, finally finding the app he's looking for. He taps it with the pen, and it opens to show another touch ID secured login page. "Damn," he mumbles through gritted teeth.

"Give it to me," I say, and this time I stride over, kneel down next to Ralph's body and as quickly as possible place the index finger onto the screen. "Here." I walk back and hand him the phone.

"Right, let's see," Oliver says and flicks through the list of passwords.

Whilst he busies himself, I exchange looks with Alice. I hold up my gloved hands, and she nods an understanding at my hint. She walks over to the utility room and rummages inside. After a minute, I see her coming out with a roll of kitchen paper and a bottle of window cleaner. Alice disappears from my view, but I hear her walking up the staircase behind me.

"Here," Oliver says. "This is it." He hands me the phone and leans over the laptop. "You'll have to read it out to me."

"Okay," I say. "Ready? Elli$01021985#," I relay, slowly reading out each letter, character and number.

He moves aside, letting me see the screen.

"What am I looking at?" I ask.

"These are the bank's capital accounts," he says. "They have set up new accounts. Looks like one for each loan Gunter has managed to obtain."

I look at the screen and there are eight accounts. The balances are shown on the right-hand side. I let out a short whistle. "He's been busy," I reply. "Which one is Alexis's?"

Oliver clicks on the account at the top. It opens up a new screen, and Oliver scrutinises the text which, consisting of numbers and letters, makes no sense to me. He does the same with the next and then the third. I can't help but feel we're losing too much time; I check to see where Alice is. I spot her crouching down near to Ralph's body, window cleaner beside her and rubbing down the chrome paperweight wrapped in kitchen paper.

"This one," Oliver says, pointing at the screen.

"Can we do a transfer online? Now?"

"I think so," Oliver says, positioning the cursor on a button with a symbol showing a box with dots in it. He clicks on it, and it opens a new window. "Looks like it," he says.

I pull out my phone and dial Alexis. He picks up immediately.

"Neil, my God, at last. How are you? What's happening? Vincent is on his way. Can you wait until he's there?" It comes out in a rush, and I have to shout to halt him.

"Alexis, I don't have time for that! I need a bank account. A safe one. Now!"

"What?"

"A bank account. Details. Now!"

"Oh, right. Hold on…" I can hear him walking fast. "I'm in my study – let me find one. Here, that'll do." He gives me the details.

"Repeat that slowly," I say, grabbing a pen and searching for a piece of paper. I find a Post-it and write down the details. I repeat them to Alexis, and he confirms. Oliver takes the Post-it from me and places it on the desk.

"So, what's happening?" Alexis asks, eager to hear the details.

"Later," I say and hang up.

I look at the screen. Oliver is typing in the details and then looks up at me.

"Do it," I say.

He clicks on the button and another screen opens up: "Enter Authorisation" it reads.

"Jeez!" I shout out. "What the hell is this?"

Oliver looks dumbfounded. "I don't know," he says. "I don't have access to these accounts. I have no idea."

"Quick, the phone," I say to him.

He picks it up, forgetting the dishcloth, and presses the button on the side. The screen comes back to life and using his finger he scrolls through the app. "Can't find anything," he says almost in a whisper as he scrolls back and forth.

"Bloody hell!" I exclaim. We got so close, but now all is lost. Quite suddenly I feel the heavy weight of defeat descending upon me. I let out my breath in a long sigh, thinking we did our best. We'll have to clear out now. We've been here too long already.

"Here, this could be it," Oliver suddenly says.

"What?"

"Here, there's an entry, but it's not connected to anything specific."

"Okay, what is it?" I say, pen poised over a new Post-it.

"AlbatrosDIII," he answers.

"You what?"

"AlbatrosDIII," he reads out once more.

"Ralph…and that fucking plane. He's really into that," I say, ripping off the rubber gloves from my sweating hands and throwing caution to the wind. I lean over the keyboard.

"No, let me," Oliver says.

"Okay, AlbatrosDIII…" I repeat.

"How many characters is that?" he asks.

"Twelve," Alice says, and I turn to look at her, surprised to find she's standing beside me, window cleaner in one hand and a bunch of kitchen paper in the other.

"A possibility?" I ask, looking at Oliver.

"Could be," he says.

"Try it," I say.

He enters the characters and presses the enter button: "Authorisation Error".

"Fuck!" I scream, frustration getting the better of me again.

"I think it's missing a special character," Oliver says. "All our passkeys have a minimum of twelve characters, of which at least one character has to be a symbol, like dollar or hashtag."

"Shit, shit, shit!" I say under my breath.

"Hold on," Alice says, and I turn to find her now holding up her smartphone. "It says here AlbatrosD.III – there's a full stop after the D. That's a special character, a symbol."

I push Oliver aside, lean over the keyboard and with utmost care type in A-l-b-a-t-r-o-s-D-.-I-I-I and press enter.

To my utter amazement the interface accepts the password.

"Confirm Transaction" the screen is now showing.

I look at Oliver again, and he nods. I click on the button and the screen blinks once, and then the message "Transaction Executed" is displayed.

We all let out a long sigh of relief, even Oliver.

"When will it be processed?" I ask.

"Overnight. First thing tomorrow it'll be on its way," Oliver replies.

"Will you intervene and stop it once we're gone?" I ask him.

He gives me a long look before answering. "No," is his one-word reply.

I scrutinise his face, looking for signs that he might be deceiving me. But I find no indication of him lying neither in his eyes nor on his face. His eyes are locked onto mine, he doesn't avert them, holding my fixed stare. "Okay," I say.

I'll have to trust him on that.

21

The monotony of the blurred landscape flashing past and the thrumming of the tyres on the tarmac sends me into a trance-like state. My mind is in a constant video loop…

Ralph lunging at me with that low animal growl.

Me shoving the crutch between his feet.

Ralph tripping, stumbling forward, his thrust deflected.

Me grabbing him and, with all the strength I could muster, propelling him over the railing.

The long drop.

I could have prevented his fall, my brain keeps saying.

But I didn't.

I *wanted* him to fall.

We're driving towards Brussels. The miles crawling by so agonisingly slowly. All I want is for this journey to end and to get home – to Zuki. The plan is for Vincent and Marcel to meet us at Brussels Airport. Alice will return the hire car and take a flight home to London.

Alice has been driving for what seems like hours. We haven't spoken a word. She has glanced across at me several times, and I know her thoughts are in turmoil, too – albeit a different turmoil to mine. We left the penthouse in a rush. I nearly forgot the crutch, remembering just in time to pick it up where it lay by the open gallery. I allowed myself one last glance down, and was surprised to see Oliver standing close by his brother, arms by his side, looking at the lifeless shape. Then a headlong rush to the lift. The agonisingly slow descent down to ground level. Nervous glances in all directions as we left the building, averting our faces as we passed pedestrians walking by. Then climbing into the car, reversing out of the parking space, and shooting off down the narrow road, Alice controlling the urge to push the accelerator right down to the metal.

***

We drive on, another hour crawls by. I sigh. A long release of air not unlike Oliver's when he first looked down from the top floor, down onto the broken, lifeless body of his brother. Alice looks across at me, startled. I look back at her. Her face shows a mix of concern and disbelief.

"I'm sorry to have dragged you into this mess," I say. The words come out heavy. It's hard to speak.

She looks away, back at the road, but turns her head to look at me once more, her eyes assessing me.

I know what she's thinking. I know the question that is burning away inside her.

"Yes, I could have prevented him from going over the railing," I say to her. "I could have prevented that fall," I admit. Our eyes meet. She turns her head back to focussing on the motorway and doesn't reply.

After a few minutes, she says, "He did lunge at you first. There was an element of self-defence in your actions. But…"

What else can she say? I could say a lot of things. I could try to justify my actions. I could try to find an excuse for killing Ralph. The blind murderous rage that burned inside me. My adrenaline-fuelled survival instincts and, I admit, my fear. But I don't. I know why I did it. He'd never have left me and Zuki, nor Alexis for that matter, in peace. A murderous enemy for life.

We sit in silence until we get to Brussels Airport. We return the hire car and watch as the man from the hire company ticks off his form. He smiles briefly at us, hovering for a few moments for a tip he doesn't get. And then he's gone. We stand facing each other.

"I'm sorry, Alice. I truly am," I say.

She looks at me intently. "But not for Ralph," she replies, half question, half statement.

"No, not for Ralph," I reply.

She looks pensive for a moment. "Not just a bad investment that," she says. Then adding after a second or two, "No, a lethal investment, that's what it was."

There's not much I can say to that, and I'm too tired anyway.

She looks at me one more time. A long look, assessing and probing at the same time. "Goodbye, Neil," she says before turning and walking away.

<h1 style="text-align:center">22</h1>

I sit in the back of the big black executive Peugeot. Cocooned within the big heavy car and its cool leather seats, I'm lost to my thoughts. Vincent and Marcel talk in hushed tones. I catch Vincent glimpsing at me in the rear mirror from time to time. He knows what's happened; Alexis has told him.

I rang Alexis after Alice left. I found a quiet spot near the terminal, telling him all, not sparing him any details. I felt he ought to know – know that I killed a man. That I did what I felt was justifiable. Justifiable to protect Zuki, him – my family.

It's a long drive to Cannes, Vincent and Marcel taking turns to drive the many miles from Brussels to Marcel's house halfway between Nice and Cannes. I can't help but feel it's ironic that I return to where everything started just over a year ago.

I'm now at Marcel's house. Not a guest but a family member. I have earnt that status and Marcel treats me with respect.

I have to wait until Alexis can sort out my return home. Taking a commercial flight is out of the question. I have no idea what's happened in the aftermath of the events in Ralph's penthouse. There's a probability that a search warrant is out for Jordan Epica. My fingerprints are on the phone and on the computer unless Oliver wiped them clean. I have no way of knowing. So, I sit and kick my heels – figuratively. My patience is wearing thin, my desire to return home, to Zuki, is overpowering. We talk on the phone constantly and whilst sparing her the grim details, she knows what's happened and my predicament.

She understands my confused state of mind. "But, darling," Zuki says for the hundredth time, "he tried to have you knocked over. And he attacked you in that penthouse. You had every right to defend yourself."

That I know, and in my mind it's not a question of whether I had a right to defend myself. It's the fact that I made a conscious decision to propel Ralph over the railing, thereby accepting the risk that he would not walk away from that fall uninjured – or walk away at all, as the case was. *That* has me searching my soul. Why did I do that? I know the answer. Because he deserved no better. Not as far as I'm concerned. He would never have stopped. He would never have stopped threatening his brother. And Julia and the kids. And he might have come for me at some point in time. And Zuki. Who knows?

"Would you have preferred it the other way round?" Zuki is asking, bringing me back from my reverie. "Just think, Neil, then it would have been little Matt or Jasmine and me having to come to terms with the void you'd have left behind."

"No, no, Zuki," I answer. "No way would I want you and little Matt *and* Jasmine having to go through life without me."

Zuki is quiet for a moment. "Did you say Matt *and* Jasmine?" she asks.

"I did," I reply, smiling to myself.

"We'll need two dolphins, then," Zuki says with a smile in her voice, referring to the small dolphin tattoos we've had done. I have mine in my groin, just above my thigh, and she has hers on her ankle.

"I have space for five or six," I say, and she laughs.

***

The days crawl by, despite the pleasant house with its swimming pool, hot tub next to the pool and outside sauna, and Marcel's doting wife, Veronique. They both take care of me, trying to make me feel comfortable and distracting me. I can't leave the house; Marcel is adamant that I need to keep low. He repeatedly says we should burn my passport – extinguish all tangible evidence of Jordan Epica ever having been real.

"No, no, Marcel," Alexis exclaims through the phone's loudspeaker as Marcel suggests once more to burn Jordan. "Neil, don't let him. I say no. We need the passport," Alexis says in a shrill voice. "We will need it for when Jordan meets his end here. Do you hear?"

Marcel does that typical French shrug – a mixture of defeat and defiance. "*Mon Dieu*, do as you like, then," he mumbles as he walks off to light the barbeque.

I laugh watching his back as he walks away, deciding to change course midway and heads to the bar first. Pastis time.

"Neil?" I hear Alexis's voice in my ear, the speaker switched off now that Marcel has left.

"Yes," I reply.

"I'll get you home soon. I promise."

"Can't wait," I say, the feeling of despair at my incarceration returning.

"Have you read the papers?" he asks, changing the topic.

"No."

"Interesting story catching on and spreading in many of them," he says.

"Is there? What are they saying?"

"There's some evidence coming to light that Ralph had amounted losses from proprietary trading – or better said, rogue trading – of over two hundred and fifty million euros. No wonder Gunter was trying so hard to get funds. Apparently, Ralph had debts everywhere. Owed a lot of money to all sorts."

"To be honest that doesn't really surprise me," I concede.

"He was high on drugs according to an interpretation of the toxicological report. They are now considering suicide, or an accident. Or an accidental suicide," he says with a short chuckle.

"Suicide?" I say, surprised at such speculation. But yes, it might explain his kamikaze lunge. Was he aiming not only to end my life but his own?

"It seems Gunter and Oliver have ensured the speculation is heading in this direction. Not that it will save the bank," Alexis says.

"Whoever investigates will see that yours were the only funds transferred out of the bank, at the time of his…*accidental suicide*."

"And they will ask themselves why Ralph did that. It was his login, his passwords. They might just think he transferred the money to an offshore account for his own purposes."

"In which case, suicide won't seem probable," I say.

"An accident, then," Alexis replies. "He was high on drugs."

Later that evening, after dinner and digestif, and with the sun beginning its fiery orange descent into the Mediterranean Sea, my phone vibrates and I check to see, expecting Zuki, but instead there's a message from Alice.

Neil. With what I've read, I can believe the suicide theory.

I wait to see if there's more coming.

He wanted to take you with him.

Another pause, and then a third message pops onto the screen.

Be a good husband and father.

Strange comment that last one, I think. But I have no issue with that. None whatsoever.

***

The private jet takes off, the pilot having briefed me when I climbed on board.

"We'll get you home in five hours," he promised with a suntanned grin and mirrored aviator's sunglasses.

I recline in the broad leather seat, stretch out my legs and once more I wonder at Alexis's resourcefulness.

"It's the least I can do," he'd said to me over the phone when informing me that a private jet would be coming to pick me up. "After all you've been through and with the twenty-five million you returned to me, Neil, it's what you deserve." He'd chuckled at that, and I wondered briefly what was so funny. "With twenty-five million spare, I might just buy the plane," he'd added.

I sat there, smiled and thought to myself that might just be a safer investment.

The End

Acknowledgements

Being a self-published author means finding the support to get the book edited, proofread, formatted and into the market. If you're lucky enough to have a publisher, many tasks are taken care of by experienced people. On your own, you take care of all this by yourself. I'd like to thank all my friends and family who have supported me. I'd also like to thank the professionals, whose services I have invested in for *A Lethal Investment*: Gary, for the structural edit; Alex, for the copy-editing and proofreading; Debbie, for the cover work.

If you enjoyed reading the book, you can support me by writing a review on Amazon or Goodreads. Your support will be very much appreciated.

For more on Alexis's and Neil's upcoming adventures please visit my website – stephenbarrettwriter.com – and sign up for the newsletters.

Manufactured by Amazon.ca
Acheson, AB